# On the Edge

A novel by

# Neal Hardin

ISBN 9781983195211

*To my sister, Margaret, brother-in-law Kevin.*

*Nephew Paul and Benita in Helsinki,*
*Finland.*

# Acknowledgement

To, my friend, Leo Batt for his advice, guidance and suggestions.

# Chapter 1

Friday 9th June.

To the untrained eye, the jumble of figures on the screen were a mass of numbers. Lots of green, yellow-white, and red. To the trained eye, the green figures represented a rising share value, yellow for no change, red for a falling value. Max Deardon took his eyes off the screen for a moment and looked at the glossy documents and the pink newspaper clippings from the Financial Times strung over his desk. Then he directed his sight through the clear glass partition that separated his office from the trading floor next door. In that room there were long rows of desks at which several dozen workers were trading stocks and shares in a frenzied high-octane environment of activity. From the trading floor he switched his eyes to look out of the window. From this vantage point, high above the City of London, he could see the spread of south London stretching far into the distance. The London skyline was forever changing. Down river, the cranes in Canary Wharf were turning. On the horizon, another office tower was nearing completion. On the other side of the river the sun was reflecting in the glass and steel structure of London's newest edition to twenty-first century architecture, the Shard.

Max Deardon's office was full of the trappings of success, like the executive toys, a big black glass-topped desk, the top-of-the-range telephone console, and the environmentally friendly PC. He worked as a market analyst for Solomon and Crew, one of the oldest firms of stockbrokers on the Square Mile. They bought and sold stocks and shares for clients, charging a fixed annual service fee. One year after the United Kingdom had voted to sever its links with the European Union, the City of London was still attracting investment despite the pessimism that prevailed about its future.

His desk lacked any picture frames holding photographs of his wife and children, because he didn't have a wife or children. He was married to the firm. She had been his wife, lover, and mistress for the past twenty years. At forty-six years of age he thought the prospect of marriage to his sometimes on-off, stop-go girlfriend, a raven-haired, thirty-something, Portuguese lady called Rosetta Sanchez, had passed him by. But stranger things had happened.

He glanced at the monitor and noted that the FTSE had closed up on a good day's trading. The Dow-Jones in New York was also up on the morning trading. The Nikkei had closed in Tokyo several hours ago, also up. The rolling news headlines flashed news of the sudden death of a much-loved and revered British TV star. He glanced into the adjoining room where the traders were beginning to wind down for the weekend. The light across the city would stay for the next three hours then the sun would begin to sink for the sunset to spread a golden sheen across the rooftops of the city.

He was just about to get up out of his chair and step to the window when the telephone on the desk sounded. By the rapid 'beep…beep…beep' coming from the contraption, he knew it was an incoming external call. He glanced at his watch. The time was ten to six.

He reached out a finger and pressed the loudspeaker button. "Max Deardon. How can I help you?" he asked.

"Max. It's Ralph," said the voice at the other end of the line.

Max recognised his brother-in-law's voice. "Ralph." he said.

"Yes."

Ralph Colby was married to Max's only sibling, his sister Helena. He had not seen or spoken to Ralph for some time, maybe six months, maybe longer.

"Hi Ralph. What can I do for you?" he asked. Colby didn't reply straight away. Maybe the question was too taxiing for him.

"It's your sister," he said.

Max was instantly alerted. "What about her?" he asked.

"She's gone missing," said Colby.

Max, now alarmed, sat forward in his seat. He knew Colby wouldn't call him if it was a trivial matter. He was a serious man who very rarely went in for light-hearted banter and jokes.

"What do you mean? Gone missing?" he asked.

"I've been meaning to tell you for a couple of days," said Colby. "She's gone."

"Gone! Gone where?" Max asked.

"I don't know," Colby replied. His voice creaked. "The truth is she's… left me," he said.

Max didn't know if he was stunned or not stunned. "What?"

"She decided to go away. A kind of split I'd guess you'd call it," said Colby. His clipped Oxford University accent didn't sound so la-di-da.

"I don't know what to say," said Max. Just then there was a knock at the door to his office. "Just a minute," he said, "I'll put you on hold."

"Yes," he called out in a raised voice. The door popped open. It was his personal assistant, a young chap called Toby Bell.

"See you next week," Toby said in a joyful demob happy way. "Have a nice weekend."

"You too," said Max. He waited for Toby to close the door, then he pressed the un-hold button. "I just don't understand," he said. "I thought you two were very happy."

"Well…" said Colby.

"Well what?"

"We've been having a difficult time recently. You know how these things are."

Max had no idea how these things were because he wasn't married.

"Where has she gone? Do you know?" he asked.

"That's just it," said Colby. "I don't know. She's taken a lot of clothing with her for a long stay. That kind of thing."

"When?"

"Oh… a few days ago," Colby said, after a hesitant pause. "I thought she'd come back, but she's still away."

"She didn't leave a forwarding address then?"

"No. Her passport isn't in the drawer. She may have left the country."

"Oh my God," said Max. He glanced into the adjoining trade floor where most of the brokers were beginning to drift towards the exit. The only traders remaining were those who did deals on the New York market. They would be here until the US market closed at eleven pm, UK time.

Colby didn't reply to his brothers-in-law's exclamation. He was perhaps waiting for a follow-up question. Something on the lines of what did he intend to do about it.

"Have you informed the police?" Max asked, then quickly added. "You've informed the police, haven't you?"

"Too early," said Colby. "She's only been gone a few days." His tone of voice did suggest he was genuinely upset that his wife of fifteen years had left the marital home, but he wasn't in major panic mode just yet.

Ralph and Helena Colby had no children. They were very successful in their fields and far too busy to have children. Ralph Colby was an orthodontist. He had a practice on Harley Street. Helena was a high-flying business consultant with clients all around the globe. The prospect and the need for children had probably never entered their heads. Though Max had detected from speaking to his sister during the past couple of years that she did have a modicum of regret that she had never had any children. Helena wasn't bad to look at. She was slim and well maintained. She had to be in the business she worked in. A high flyer. A career-driven type who had a thick-list of clients here in the UK and further afield. Ralph was fifty-one years of age. Helena was forty-three.

Max didn't know what to say. This news had come unexpectedly. He couldn't comprehend that his sister had left Colby. After all a martial problem was something he never had to deal with and frankly the state of his sister's marriage had little to do with him. He had never questioned them before and didn't want to start now.

"Thanks for letting me know," he said. "You'll keep me posted if she returns or if you hear from her. Won't you?"

"Of course. I will. You'll let me know if she contacts you."

"Of course," said Max.

"So, long."

"Bye," said Max.

The severing of the line made a solid click. Max couldn't do a thing. He got up out of his seat, stepped to the solid-plate window and looked out over the city and down to the streets of the square mile. The early evening sunlight was bathing the buildings and the streets that were gridlocked. Over on London Bridge the stream of human traffic was heading across the pavements and scurrying towards the railway station like a stream of ants.

He wondered why Ralph had called to tell him. Maybe it was to pre-empt him. Max usually spoke to his sister on the telephone at least once a month. He was due to call her in the next couple of days. Colby must have been calling him before he called her. This way, Max couldn't accuse him of not caring. To prevent this Colby had called him first.

He returned to his desk, sat in his high-backed leather chair and tried to think straight. Ralph Colby was an okay type of guy, hardworking, motivated, profit driven. There was nothing wrong with that. His practice, which went by the name of, 'The Belgravia Dental Implant Studio' was on Harley Street where the great and the good in any medical profession had their practice. Colby's clients ranged from stars of screen and TV to people in sport, fashion and music. He never bragged about his client list, but he certainly knew some movers and shakers, from members of parliament to up-and-comers in the pop industry. Any scandal about his marriage would be very embarrassing and not very welcome.

Max didn't believe that Ralph would have harmed his sister or even wished her any ill will, but something wasn't quite right. He had grown closer to Helena since the passing of his parents who died within two months of each other six years ago. They spoke on the telephone and saw each other once or twice every eight weeks or thereabouts.

He had an idea. He looked through his contacts on his phone, found Helena's smart phone number and called it. The dialling tone rang for a minute, then it went to voice mail. He said: 'Hi Helena, it's Max. If you get this message, please give me a call. I've just spoken to Ralph. I understand that you've left him.' He ended the call, then wished he hadn't said the last two sentences. Too late. The message was waiting in her in-box.

It occurred to Max that in the seventeen or so years he had known Ralph Colby he hadn't talked to him at length, one to one, on no more than half a dozen occasions. Indeed, if you had to count the number of times they had chatted for more than ten minutes at one time then he would only require the fingers of one hand. In truth, he didn't know him that well. He knew that he was motivated by profit, and could be a condescending prat, but other than that he didn't know him at all. It was an admission that got him thinking about their relationship, which wasn't bad, but they weren't exactly buddies.

# Chapter 2

Max Deardon hadn't heard a thing from either his sister or his brother-in-law for five days. Nothing had happened in the interim to tell him that his sister had returned to their home in the Berkshire countryside or their flat in the Barbican complex.

He was in his office, high above the streets of central London. The sunshine of last week had given way to a period of changeable weather and a stiff, easterly breeze was ruffling the surface of the Thames.

The time was nearly twelve noon. Max had just chaired a meeting of colleagues to discuss the strategy going forward to the second quarter of the financial year. The stock market had taken a hit in the past few days at the news of less than expected growth in the US manufacturing sector. Stocks were in decline, though still buoyant when compared to this time last year when the Brexit result had become a reality.

Max turned his attention back to his sister and brother-in-law. Ralph was either seeking to play-down her disappearance or he had something to hide, though Max had no reason to suspect anything untoward. In truth, he liked Colby though he could at times be high-handed and supercilious. Behind the rich professional image, he liked to convey to the outside world and his clients, he had an edge and a kind of Doctor Jekyll and Doctor Hyde temperament and personality. Although Colby was pleasant and personable Max did have mixed feelings about him, but maybe that was down to the fact that he was his sister's husband. He had an idea. He would visit Colby and try to see him in his Harley Street studio.

It was just after three in the afternoon when Max left his office and headed over to Marylebone which wasn't a million miles away from the City. He took a black cab to Harley Street.

Ralph Colby's dental implant studio was in a four-story property in a long block of buildings between Devonshire Street and Weymouth Street. Top-of-the-range-cars lined the street. Colby had the entire ground floor of the property to himself. There was a beauty salon on the first floor and a business selling herbal remedies on the second. The top floor was currently vacant.

Max stepped up the steps to the front door, then through the door and into a marble walled vestibule. Access to the inner area was barred by a stout-looking walnut and glass door. An intercom unit was imbedded into the wall. A plaque attached to the wall gave the details of each of the practices in the building. It indicated that the ground floor was occupied by, 'The Belgravia Implant Studio', Doctor R. G. Colby-Lewis, then a series of letters after his name, along with details of the membership of this and that institution.

He glanced out of the door onto the pathway as a pedestrian sauntered by the entrance. The day had turned warmer than it had been at seven-thirty that morning when he arrived for work. The air tasted thick with the exhaust fumes that were been pumped out of the traffic on the nearby Euston Road.

Max pushed on the door, but it was locked so he pressed the button marked #1 in the intercom. A CCTV camera was pointing down to the doorstep. A click came out of the intercom unit.

"Hello. How can I help you?" asked a female voice.

"I'd like to see Doctor Colby-Lewis," Max said. Ralph did have a double-barrelled name, though Max seldom used the Lewis extension.

"Do you have an appointment?" the lady asked.

"No. But I'd like to speak to Ralph. He's my bother-in-law," Max said as if this would get him instant access to the inner sanctum.

"He's with a client right now," she said.

"I can wait."

She didn't reply immediately. He waited for the door to buzz open. "What's your name?" she asked.

"Max Deardon."

"One moment please."

One moment, turned into one minute before she came back over the air.

"Hello. I've spoken to Mr Colby-Lewis," she said. "He can see you for five minutes. Please come in."

Before he could say thanks, there was a buzz, then the clunk of a lock opening. Max pushed the door open and stepped into a marble-floored area with an elegant staircase snaking up the wall on the left and an elevator on the other side. Directly ahead was a semi-opaque glass door with the words: 'The Belgravia Implant Studio' stencilled on it in fancy gold-lettered font.

He took the handle, pushed it down and entered a five-sided waiting room that had alternate, floor to ceiling, walnut, and tiffany glass panels. Solid leather armchairs were set against three of the sides. Several pots of plants were placed on three waist-high tables. A central table had the ubiquitous array of glossy lifestyle magazines spread across it. The air was odourless

A single door opened and a rather attractive young lady, who was wearing a white jacket and matching trousers appeared. She smiled at him.

"Please take a seat. Mr Colby-Lewis will be with you shortly," she said.

Through the door Max could hear the whirr of a machine, then a voice that sounded like his brother-in-law talking to a third person.

Max took a seat and looked round the interior. He surmised there would be another entrance and exit at the back, for those who didn't want to be seen entering or leaving the studio by the front door. For some of his clients were top-list celebrities, who perhaps didn't want to be seen entering a dental studio. For now, he set his eyes on a TV screen that was showing a promotional video of the 'before and after' pictures of a man, flanked by a besotted lady, who in the after-surgery shots was smiling and showing off his new teeth. Little doubt that the price for a full set of new pearly whites would run well into the fifty-thousand-pound bracket. Max snuggled into the seat and waited.

The last time he had spent any quality time with both Helena and Ralph was Boxing Day two years ago. He recalled the day vividly. It had been a joyous occasion. Rosetta had accompanied him to their Berkshire home. Helena and he had reminisced about the Christmases they had when they were kids. The age gap of only three years meant they were close and shared many experiences of growing up together. Like the time it had snowed on Christmas day and their late father had taken them sledging on a local field next to their home. These were the precious moments. The memories of years past. He remembered the first Christmas gift he had bought her using the pennies he had saved in a piggy-bank. It was a knitted rag-doll he had bought from a charity shop. He must have been six years of age, Helena was only three. She had that ragdoll for years. It may have lost an eye and the stuffing had gone limp, but she still had the doll for years until it became too worn to keep. He smiled to himself as he recalled those times. They were what made life so fascinating.

Thirty minutes passed. No one came into the waiting room. The sound of Colby's voice had tailed off some time ago along with the sound of the drill. Max could feel his eyes becoming heavy. He had left home for work at six forty-five that morning. The time was now getting on for four o'clock. Outside the evening rush-hour was beginning to take hold. He closed his eyes and felt himself drifting off when the door leading into the studio opened and Ralph Colby emerged with a man who looked to be of either Indian or Arab background. The man glanced at Max, ever so briefly, then he took Colby's offered hand and they exchanged a hand shake. "I'll see you again in six months," said Colby.

Colby had that moral and ethical assurance about him. A perfect customer-oriented manner. He was a distinguished looking man. Six feet tall, tanned, and bright eyed. He would work on his appearance with Botox and all the latest creams and potions, though he'd deny it.

In a white jacket, salmon coloured shirt and silk tie he looked stylish. The words: Belgravia Dental Studio, Dr R.G. Colby-Lewis were embroidered into the top of a breast pocket in red silk thread. He was okay looking. Charming smile. A whiff of wealth and sophistication about him. He told Max that he was from Oxford, but Max had his doubts. He thought his Oxford accent was manufactured. His hair which was starting to thin on the top of his crown was lightly oiled. He had that sense of direction of an actor playing a part. He led his client to the door, opened it and took him out into the vestibule.

He returned almost immediately and approached Max to shake hands.

"Max. What a nice surprise," he said. He grinned or maybe it was a genuine smile. Max couldn't tell which. Although, they were brothers-in-law, they rarely saw each other, particularly over the last couple of years. When Helena came into town to have lunch with Max, she was usually on her own.

In the time Max had last seen him in the flesh, Colby hadn't changed at all. He was still tall and slender, though his thatch of hair was showing signs of greying at the temples and becoming wispy at the summit.

"Come through," he said. He led Max through the door, down an enclosed corridor with a closed door at the bottom. A door to the right, leading into one of the studios was open. Max glanced in to see Colby's pretty female assistant bending over to put something into a long drawer in a unit. The room was full of the usual dental paraphernalia.

Colby carried on along the corridor to the door at the bottom, opened it and led him into his office. The room was in the shape of a hexagon. A pair of old-style, free-standing, tall, glass-door cabinets were set against two walls. A pair of French windows led out onto a patio and garden. There was a desk on one side. Frames displaying diplomas, photographs of Colby with some influential people were on the wall behind his desk, but none of his wife. The desk had a leather inlay cover. It looked classical French with bowed legs and a carved pattern.

Colby sat behind the desk in a leather chair and surveyed all before him. He gestured to the client's seat at the other side of the desk. The white jacket with his name on it, gave him the look of some big-league surgeon, but that is what he was. He removed people's teeth then filled their mouth with a fresh set. He wasn't cheap. By the look of the top-of-the-range telephone unit and the PC, he was doing okay for himself. He was a highly motivated guy. Max had always thought that from the moment he met him about twenty years ago. Then he was just a normal dentist with his own private practice in North London. Now he was a highly skilled and much sought-after orthodontist.

He looked at Max, then took in a deep intake of oxygen and adjusted his posture.

Max began. "She's still not back then?" he asked.

"No."

"Why did she go?" Max asked.

"Simple. We had a falling out. Nothing too drastic."

"Do you know where she's gone?"

"I don't know," Colby replied.

"It's unlike Helena," Max said. "She's precise. I would have thought she would have at least given you a forwarding address. She was always thoughtful like that when we were kids. I don't think she's changed all that much."

"Well that's the way it is," replied Colby in a stiff, brusque manner. He'd maintained eye contact with his brother-in-law and his face locked in a gaze, as if he was in a blinking contest with him.

"She hasn't called me," said Max.

Colby shrugged his shoulders. His body language was closed, and he wasn't breathing in deeply or rapidly as if he was lying or under stress.

"To be honest. She's been gone longer than the period I initially told you. It's nearer to three weeks," he admitted.

Max was stunned by this revelation. "Three weeks ago!" he exclaimed. "You said she'd been gone for a couple of days. Not weeks."

Colby sat forward and rested his forearms on the leather inlay cover. "I didn't want to alarm you," he said.

"Alarm me! Are you kidding? She's been gone for three weeks. Have you called the police?"

"No," said Colby.

"Why not?" asked Max demanding to know.

"Why? Why should I? She's over twenty-one years of age," he said in a dismissive manner. "If she's gone. She's gone. The police aren't going to do anything. Why should they? She took enough clothes with her to last a year. She took her passport, and make-up and other things. She's a grown woman who can think and act for herself," Colby said raising his voice a notch.

"But…" said Max, then stopped himself. Colby had a very good point. Helena was an adult who could look after herself. If she had gone because of an argument and left under her own free will, then there wasn't a great deal he could do. The police wouldn't have taken much interest, unless there was a clear indication of foul-play, which he assumed there wasn't.

"Has this happened before?" Max asked.

"What?" replied Colby.

"Her going."

"She once went for a week without telling me where she'd gone," Colby said.

"When?"

"Several years ago."

"But never as long as three weeks?" Max queried.

"Never as long as three weeks," Colby agreed.

"So, her going off for periods of time isn't uncommon?"

Colby pursed his lips. "I wouldn't say it's common. She has gone before, but not for this length of time," he admitted.

"What was the argument about?" Max asked. He knew that Colby didn't have to answer the question if he didn't want to.

"Nothing much," he sighed. "It was about whether to put the apartment in the Barbican up for sale, to finance an extension of the studio business to other cities in the country."

"Is that all?" Max asked.

"That's all," Colby said. He sat back, took a shallow breath, and rested his arms on the armrests of his chair.

Max looked at him. He seemed cocksure in his answer, so he had little ammunition to pursue this line of questioning.

Just then the telephone on the desk sounded and Colby answered it. "Thank you," he said, then he put the telephone down. "My next client is here," he said, which was code for him to get to his feet. "I'll keep you informed if she gets in touch," he said.

Max got up out of the seat. Colby led him through the door, along the corridor, and passed the door to the studio which was now closed. He escorted him back into the waiting room where a pretty lady and a man were sitting close together in adjoining seats.

"Nice to see you, Max," said Colby. "I'll be in touch shortly should there be a change of circumstances. I wouldn't worry too much. I'm sure there'll be a perfectly good outcome in a short while."

He offered his hand to Max. He took it, shook hands with his brother-in-law and promptly left the building and stepped out into the late afternoon light. Notwithstanding Colby's assurances, he was concerned. He was so concerned that within seconds of stepping out into the sunlight he decided to contact the police to report a missing person.

# Chapter 3

Max Deardon was back in his office high above the streets of central London for a quarter to five. Colleagues on the trading floor were reflecting on a quiet day's trading. The main news of the day had been an announcement by Her Majesty's Treasury for plans going forward for Brexit. They had proposed a plan to reduce some regulations in order to encourage investors to stay in London. This initiative had resulted in a small increase to the FTSE index, though it was starting to drop back a touch as trading was about to close.

Max logged onto his PC. He did a Google search for the Metropolitan Police missing person bureau. He couldn't find a link, so he picked up the telephone and tapped in the number for the main Scotland Yard switchboard.

After hitting a few dead-ends he was put through to a unit in a police station in Holborn. A female officer answered the call and asked him how she could help him. He said he wanted to report his sister missing. The WPC took his telephone number and asked him for details of her name and other items of information like her age and address, which he gave to her. She told him that someone would call him back shortly. Max was reticent to end the conversation, because he assumed no one would call him back.

It was another twenty minutes before his telephone rang. By the rapid bleep pattern, he knew it was an incoming external call. He hit the loudspeaker button and introduced himself.

"Is that Max Deardon?" asked a female voice.

"Yes."

"My name is DI Eileen Welsh. I understand that you want to report your sister missing."

"That's correct."

"What's her name?" she asked.

"Helena Colby. Colby-Lewis if your using the correct name, but she doesn't use the Lewis part."

"Is it Colby or Colby-Lewis?" DI Welsh asked with a tiny hint of impatience in the tone of her voice.

"Colby."

"How long has she been missing?"

"Over three weeks."

"Is your sister married?"

"Yes."

"Why hasn't her partner reported her as missing?"

"Because, according to him, she's left him," he replied.

"So, she's not really missing then?"

"She's missing because she hasn't contacted him or me to tell us where she is."

"Does she usually tell you where she is?"

"No, but…"

"No, but what?"

"No, but I would have expected her to have contacted me by now to tell me where she is."

"Does your sister often go missing?"

"According to him, it's not unusual," he replied.

"If she left of her own free will then she's not really missing, is she?"

"That's what he said."

"Who?"

"Her husband," Max replied with a nip in his voice. He was becoming impatient with the tone and direction of her questions.

DI Welsh asked him if he believed her husband. He said he didn't know. She asked him for her husband's full name, his age and address. When he told her, they lived in a house in the Berkshire countryside and had a flat in the Barbican she asked him if they were well-to-do.

Max was going to ask what had that got to do with anything but thought better of it. "He's an implant dentist and she's a business consultant," he replied.

"Does she work away a lot?" she asked.

"Yes."

"Maybe she's away on a business assignment," she speculated.

"If that's the case, why would he tell me she's left him. I'm nervous. Something isn't right."

"Why do you say that?"

"It's just not like her to leave without telling me."

"But she's done it before. Did she tell you then?"

"No. But she's not been gone for this length of time without telling me."

"She hasn't called you before when she's gone. That's what you said."

"That's true," he replied.

"How many times have they split up in the past?"

"I'm not sure."

"Has her partner got any record of violence towards her?" she asked.

"I don't think so. He doesn't seem like the type."

"What type is that?"

"He's a successful dentist with a practice on Harley Street," he replied.

DI Welsh didn't reply for a few long moments. She must have been filtering his answers and trying to make some sense of them.

"I'll tell you what we'll do," she said. "We'll make a note of it. What I suggest is that you give it another week at least and…."

"Another week," he said cutting her off in mid-sentence. "That will make it almost a month."

"Give it another week," she repeated.

"I'm reluctant to do that," he replied. "Is there anything else, I can do?"

"There's nothing that I can suggest to you. At the moment there's nothing to indicate that she's come to any harm or that she's been kidnapped. If she has left, her partner of her own free will it might be that she's just staying away and waiting for things to smooth over."

"I'm not so sure," said Max. "I'm not convinced all is well."

"Okay. We can speak to her husband and get his side of the story, but you'll probably discover that she's fine. Maybe she doesn't want to speak to anyone just yet," she said.

"Yeah, but it's almost four weeks."

"Four weeks is no time," she said in a dismissing tone. "We've had people returning after...oh...four, five, six months."

"Hmmm," said Max under his breath. He wanted to say that that wasn't his sister, but he held back.

"We'll give her partner a call."

The call ended after less than four minutes. He wondered what to do next. He had an idea. He made an internal call to talk to a chap called Lloyd Sherwood.

# Chapter 4

Lloyd Sherwood was the nearest thing Max Deardon had to what could be termed, a genuine friend, in the company. Sherwood's title was 'Head of Corporate Security'. Max asked him if he wouldn't mind popping into this office for a chat. It shouldn't take a couple of minutes. Lloyd said okay.

Lloyd Sherwood was a company man. He had grown up with the organisation. Man, and boy. His service record was longer than Deardon's. He was perhaps one of the longest- serving employees of the three hundred, or so, staff in the London office. Lloyd had started at the company as a messenger boy in the post-room, then over the next twenty-five years he had advanced up the pyramid to become Head of Security. Not bad for a Brixton boy. If anyone asked him where he had been educated, he would say *the U of L*. Oh, the University of London, people would ask. No, the University of Life, he would reply with his tongue firmly in his cheek. His nickname was *Studious Sherwood* or *Sharp*, because he was as sharp as the blade of a cut-throat.

His job was to keep tabs on all the trading floor employees to ensure no one stepped out of line. Max liked him. He was hard, but fair and good at what he did.

A couple of minutes passed since the call had ended, when there was a knock at the door. "Come in," shouted Max. The door opened, and Lloyd came in. At around five foot eleven tall and adequately bulky he cut the image of a man who knew how to look after himself. He sat in the chair by the side of Max's desk and rested his right forearm on the table top.

"I've got a problem," said Max.

"I wouldn't have thought you've asked me to see you at ten past six in the evening to discuss the latest football transfer rumours," he said.

Max smiled at the quip. "I'll cut to the quick," he said. "My sister, Helena, has gone missing. She left her husband about four weeks ago. I went to see him today. He says he doesn't have a clue where she is."

"It isn't the first time, is it?" Lloyd queried.

"How do you know that?"

"Let's just call it a lucky guess."

"No. She's done it before. But she hasn't been gone for this length of time."

"You're concerned, aren't you?" Lloyd said.

"Does it show?" Max asked. Lloyd didn't answer him. Max continued. "Yes. I'm concerned. I would have thought she would have contacted me by now, but I haven't heard a thing from her."

"I guess you keep in touch with her regularly?" Lloyd asked.

"Yeah. We've grown closer since the death of our parents."
Lloyd nodded his head. "Is there anything you can suggest to help
me find her?" Max asked.

Lloyd ran the tip of his thumb over the heel of his chin and
blew out a long breath. His face was studied in thought. "Well, there
is," he said.

"What?" asked Max.

"You could consider hiring a private detective to find her."

Max glanced up at the ceiling. "Why didn't I think of that?"
he said. He shifted his position in his seat. "Good idea. But who? Do
you know anyone who fits the bill?"

"I know a Private Eye. His name is Steve Chilton. He's got a
place in Soho. He does enquiries of this nature. If he can't find her
no one can," Lloyd revealed. "If you want I can ask him on your
behalf. If I make the enquiry, it will keep you out of the loop. But
beware he won't be cheap. He's expensive," he warned.

"No expense spared. Not where my sister is concerned. She's
my only flesh and blood," Max said.

He glanced towards the window and the view overlooking
the city, then through the glass partition. The trading floor was
empty, but for a crew of a dozen brokers who were tracking activity
on the Dow-Jones in New York City and taking calls from clients.

"Do you want me to contact him?" Lloyd asked.

Max thought about the question for a second. "Yeah. Lets do that."

"Best if we keep it secret," said Lloyd. He wasn't called *studious Sherwood* for nothing.

"Of course," said Max. "I wouldn't like anything like this to get out to the senior management team." He tilted his head upward to indicate those one floor up. "God knows they've got their hands full of other important things," he said referring to the ramifications of Brexit.

Lloyd made a whimsical face and nearly laughed out loud. "Perhaps you'd better fill me in," he said. "Names and details and things like that."

"My brother-in-law is Ralph Colby-Lewis. I only know him as Ralph Colby. I very rarely use the Lewis part. He contacted me last Friday evening. Told me that my sister had gone. That she'd taken some clothes and those kind of items."

"Passport?" Lloyd asked.

"Yeah. That as well."

"Any money?"

"Yeah. Probably."

"What's does Colby do for a living?" Lloyd asked.

"He's one of those posh dentists who does implants and all that kind of thing."

"Where?" Lloyd asked.

"He's got a studio on Harley Street. Charges top dollar. He's got a client list that reads like who's hot. And who wants to be a celebrity."

Lloyd chewed on his top lip for a few brief moments. "Has he got a bit on the side?" he asked.

"Who Ralph? A mistress?"

"Yeah, that kind of thing. A lover? A girlfriend?"

"Not that I'm aware of," Max replied.

"How old is he?" Lloyd asked.

"Fifty-one. Helena is forty-four. No, forty-three," he corrected.

"What's he like?" Lloyd asked.

"To look at?"

"No. Character. Traits. That kind of thing."

"Solid. Hard working. He's done very well for himself."

"Any children?"

"None."

"Free birds then?"

"You could say that," Max replied.

"No tie-ups of any kind?"

"None that I know of."

"What reason did he give you for her going?" Lloyd asked.

"Said they'd had an argument about whether to put their Barbican flat on the market, and use the money to expand his practice," Max replied.

"It doesn't seem like a legitimate reason why anyone would walk out."

"That's what I thought," said Max.

"If it was something like an extra marital affair, then I could understand it. Something about selling a flat sounds a bit flaky to me," Lloyd remarked.

"I think you're right," said Max. "That's why I want to know what-in-God's name is going on. That's what I told the police."

"You've spoken to the police?" Lloyd asked.

"Yes. On the telephone."

"Who did you speak to?"

"A DI Welsh in Holborn. A female detective."

"What did she advise?"

"That I give it another week. She did say they would speak to Ralph to get his side of the story, to assess if any bells and whistles go off."

"Did you say you've seen him today?" Lloyd asked.

"Yeah. In the past couple of hours at his place of work."

"How was he?"

"Seemed genuine at first. Then a little dismissive towards the end of our conversation."

"Who are his clients?" Lloyd asked.

"TV and film stars. Sportsmen and women. Models. Pop tarts."

Lloyd smiled at the last remark, then nodded his head as if he knew who he was talking about. "As he contacted the police? Given them her description?" he asked.

"No."

"You say they've got a place in the Barbican. Have they got another home?" Lloyd asked.

"A big house out in Berkshire, just this side of Reading. He only goes home on weekends. He doesn't work on a Friday."

"Could she be there?" Lloyd asked.

"Doubt it," said Max. "Anyway, she would have contacted me by now," he added.

"Have you tried her mobile phone? A text? An email? Facebook? Twitter? That kind of thing?"

"All of those," said Max. "No answer to any."

Lloyd sat back in the seat. He took his arm off the table and held it across his chest. There was a tiny glint of perspiration on his face. "Leave it with me," he said. "I'll act as the go-between. Is there anything else I need to know?" he asked.

"Don't think so. Will I have to meet this guy?" Max asked.

"Not if you don't want to," said Lloyd. "Or unless he specifically wants to talk to you," he added. Max didn't reply. "I'll contact Chilton this evening. Get the ball rolling. I'll let you know when he comes up with something."

Lloyd pushed the chair back and got to his feet. He glanced at the clock. The time was twenty-three minutes past six.

"Thanks," said Max.

"No problem," said Lloyd. "I'm sure we'll get to the bottom of it in no time. Maybe she's jetted off to the South of France or Barbados for a long break."

"Yeah, more than likely," said Max, trying to match Lloyd's up-beat assessment. He watched Lloyd go to the door, open it and step out onto the corridor.

That evening Max left the office at six-forty-five in the knowledge that he was finally getting somewhere, but unsure of what the outcome would be.

He was home in his Swiss Cottage flat by seven-thirty. The evening was warm and pleasant. The pretty girls in their shorts and skimpy tops, loitering around the stores along Finchley Road made him reflect on his sometimes girlfriend Rosetta. He would have loved to have seen her this evening. Alas, she was back home in Lisbon visiting her parents. Unfortunately, her father had been taken ill in the past few weeks, hence her decision to go home to see her parents. In the event, it was in some ways a good job he had turned down the invitation to accompany her. His excuse was that he was too busy at work.

He acknowledged to himself that their relationship was nothing short of a casual soft romance. Often captured in one of those instantly forgettable Rom-com movies in which one partner is mad keen on the other, but the other doesn't share the same sentiments until some traumatic event or fate brings them closer together. He didn't know if he was the one who was lukewarm, or if it was her. Or if she was mad keen on him but playing it coy in case he called it off.

He had met her about two years ago when a delegation from the recently opened Lisbon office had visited London for a training event. In the evening, Max and several of his senior management colleagues had played host to their Portuguese colleagues and taken them to a West-End restaurant for dinner. Max was immediately attracted to Rosetta's silky dark looks, charming smile and quiet personality. He thought she wouldn't be interested in a dinosaur like him. The following day at the training event he plucked up the courage to ask her out, she agreed. That evening he took her to dinner, then to a traditional London pub for drinks. She said she wanted to experience a typical East-End public-house, so he took her to a place he knew in Bow. Close to the St Mary-le-Bow church from where Bow bells chimed the hour. They got on fine and established a good rapport. The following day she returned to Lisbon with her colleagues. He vowed to keep in touch with her, then less than two months later Rosetta applied for and got a job in London with another firm. She gave Max her new address and he helped her to move in. One thing led to another. They began to see each other on a regular basis and their love blossomed, but then it stalled like an old banger of a car trying to get up a steep hill. It became nothing more than an on-off, casual relationship.

Max often wondered about attempting to take it to the next level and ask her to move in with him, but he didn't make the move. Still there was time to do so.

The next day was Thursday. He wasn't due into the office this weekend. He was planning to have a relaxing weekend, as relaxing as he could with his sister missing for one day short of four weeks. As the head of the family he felt a moral duty to locate her. Like it was something he needed to do not only to try and find her but also because in a subconscious way he wanted to delve deeper into his brother-in-law's psyche and discover something about him that would give him leverage over him. Something he could use if his brother-in-law ever came after him.

Thursday came and went. Friday passed, and the weekend came around. Max spent most of the time in the communal garden taking in the rays. He received an email from Rosetta to tell him how she was getting on in Lisbon. Sadly, her father's condition had deteriorated to the point where he had been placed in an intensive care unit. Max replied, saying he was thinking about her. He asked her to pass on his regards and best wishes to her family. He choose not to mention anything about his sister's disappearance.

# Chapter 5

Monday 19<sup>th</sup> June

On Monday morning, there was an unexpected development in the case. Within minutes of getting to work at eight o'clock, Max received a telephone call from DI Eileen Welsh. She requested that he visit her in a police station on Theobald's Street in Holborn. She told him that the police had conducted a telephone interview with Ralph Colby over the weekend. She had an update to give him, but, ironically, she didn't want to divulge the content to him over the telephone. Max agreed to meet her later in the afternoon, once the Far East markets had closed for the day.

It was getting on for three o'clock when he left the office. He took a cab into Holborn and made his way onto Theobald's Street. The police station in Holborn was a reasonable-sized building on a busy thoroughfare, but the kind of place you wouldn't notice if you weren't looking for it.

A Metropolitan police emblem and lantern hung over the entrance doorway. He entered the interior and headed for the counter in a light-filled space. An air conditioning unit was blowing cool air around the reception area and there was a strong smell of a cleaning fluid.

A young female officer in uniform was standing at the counter, looking over some papers or other. She raised her head and eyed the member of the public in her midst.

"Hello," she said. "How can I help you?" she asked in a nice easy-going tone.

"My name is Max Deardon. I've come to meet DI Welsh," he said.

She took a telephone from under the counter and tapped in a three-digit number into the face, then she spoke.

"There is a visitor. Mr Deardon, to see you," she said. She listened to DI Welsh's response, then put the telephone down. "Wait here," she said. "She'll be with you in a moment." He smiled and thanked her.

A minute passed before a solid wood and glass door on the left opened and a woman in a black trouser-suit emerged. She was perhaps in her forties, not tall, a little over five feet two inches in height, frumpy-looking, bordering on mildly obese. Her hair wasn't styled or if it was she needed to book an appointment to give it some bounce. She was hardly like one of the glamorous lady detectives you see on TV these days. She was holding a manila folder under her arm which wasn't very thick, perhaps it was a transcript of an interview they had had with Ralph Colby.

She raised her head and looked at him. No trace of a smile on her lips. The phone behind the counter rang. The WPC answered it.

"Mr Deardon?" the woman enquired. He stepped close to the counter. It was then that he saw the name badge attached to the lapel of her jacket, *DI Eileen Welsh, M.P.U.* which must have stood for, 'Missing Person's Unit.'

"Yes," he replied.

"I'm DI Eileen Welsh. It's nice to meet you," she said. She didn't have a London accent, possibly North-East England or someplace up there.

She stepped through an open hatch in the counter and came through to his side. "Perhaps you'd like to follow me," she said. He followed her through the reception area to where it narrowed to a corridor, then down the corridor, through an open door and into a small interview room. The room was windowless. An open air-duct in the wall allowed fresh air to come in and circulate. There was a table and two chairs on one side. She elected not to close the door behind her.

She slipped into a hard-backed, black plastic seat at one side of the table, then gestured for him to do likewise. He did as she requested. He could smell her tangy fragrance. He observed her small, podgy fingers open the manila folder. She looked at the top sheet. The folder only contained a few pages. She raised her head and gave him a brief smile. There was no sound, except for the faint noise of the traffic on the road outside.

"We interviewed your brother-in-law, Ralph Colby-Lewis, about the disappearance of your sister," she said. "He said she went out of her own free will, because she's left him for someone else. Someone she met on a business trip to Paris."

Max's mouth fell open. This revelation stunned him. He recovered his composure. "He never told me that," he said.

"Perhaps he was too embarrassed to discuss it with you. Who wants to admit that his wife has found someone else?" she asked. Her accent was definitely North of England. Maybe West Yorkshire. Leeds at a guess.

Max reflected on her words for a few brief moments. "That's a fair point," he admitted. "If that's what he told you, then perhaps it's true. But it still doesn't answer the question of why she hasn't been in touch with me," he said.

"Perhaps *she's* too embarrassed," said DI Welsh. She certainly had all the answers. Maybe she was being a little dismissive, but she must have considered all the possible variables.

"Maybe," said Max.

"She's human," said DI Welsh.

Max adjusted his posture. The hard surface of the seat was digging into the back of his knees. He didn't reply to her, so she continued.

"How often do you see your sister?"

"Not that often," he admitted.

"So, she never had the chance to mention it to you?"

"No. Why would she?" he asked.

"Exactly. Why would she?"

"Okay, she's got another man. It still doesn't answer the question of why she hasn't been in touch."

Now it was her turn to scowl. "I think we've established the possibility of why that's the case," she said.

"What are you going to do about it?" he asked.

"About what?" she asked.

"Finding my sister," he replied.

"There is absolutely no evidence or suggestion of foul-play. Nothing to suggest that your sister has come to any harm. Mr Colby didn't give us any cause to be alarmed. She could be with this new man in a love nest for all you know," she said in a quick tone that got stronger and louder towards the end.

"That's true," he admitted.

DI Welsh closed the manila file and laid her hand flat on the top as if she had no intention of ever opening the file again.

"Thank you for coming to see me," she said. "We have an open mind about your sister, but nothing we've learned has given us any cause for further investigation. If that situation changes, you'll be the first to know."

She put her hands down flat on the table top, pushed the chair back and pulled herself up. She held her hand out, fingers together and stiff. He got to his feet and took her hand. She had quite a firm grip. She was straight, but butch with it. The ring on her wedding finger suggested that she was in a male-female relationship. But who knew for sure? He didn't care.

Max thanked her for taking his enquiry seriously and for interviewing Colby. At least Colby now knew that he was looking out for his sister. The story about her leaving him because she had a new man might be genuine. Colby was a proud man. Maybe he had been too embarrassed to reveal the truth. It still didn't explain why she hadn't contacted him to tell him.

# Chapter 6

Tuesday 20th June

On Tuesday morning, Max was called into a meeting with his boss and six other members of the Senior Management team. The Chief Executive Officer of the firm was a formidable lady by the name of Petra DeVries. The Head of Human Resource, Sara Lynn, was also in attendance. The news wasn't great. He'd had better. But it wasn't totally unexpected.

Petra DeVries addressed the seven members of the management team. She told them that the owners were seeking to cut costs to increase profit. Their method was to *let people go* or in other words senior management jobs were on the line. Or maybe the better expression for Max was that his job was *on the edge'*. There had been hints of something in the air with the news that a party of senior people from the parent company, based in Zurich, was on the prowl looking over the books.

DeVries told everyone that a very generous redundancy package was available to all management-level members of staff at a certain salary scale who wished to apply for it. When taking his age and years of service into account, Max thought he could walk away with a cheque for around two million pounds tax free if he applied for voluntary redundancy. Not everyone who applied was guaranteed to be accepted. Now he had to weigh-up if it was worthwhile to apply for the package or to hang-on with the possibility that he would be made redundant and lose the half a million pounds incentive the company were dangling as a carrot. The dilemma took his mind off his missing sister for the remainder of the day.

Wednesday 21st June.

Lloyd Sherwood came to see Max just before the close of play on the trading floor. It had been a week since he had called him to discuss the matter. Lloyd made himself comfortable in the chair aside of Max's desk. He looked serious.

"What've you got?" Max asked him.

"After we chatted, I contacted Steve Chilton of Chilton Private Investigation and put him on the case."

"What's he found?" Max asked. He expected him to say *not a lot*.

"Plenty."

"Plenty? Like what?"

Lloyd ran the tip of his tongue along his top lip. "Are you ready for this?" he said.

"Ready for what?"

There was a glow in Lloyd's eyes. "He said that your brother-in-law knows some people."

"What kind of people?" Max asked, flummoxed.

"People like Lomax and Delaney."

"Who the hell are Lomax and Delaney?"

"Eric Lomax and Louis Delaney."

"I don't know anyone of that name."

"Of course, you don't," said Lloyd.

"Who are they?" Max asked.

"A pair of well-known South London criminals. They head a group of would be gangsters who are into all sorts of criminal activity," Lloyd said.

"You're kidding?"

"No. Really."

"Crime. Like what?"

"Drug dealing, money laundering, fencing stolen gold bullion. That kind of thing," Lloyd replied.

"Geez. And Ralph Colby knows these people?"

"That's the information he's got," said Lloyd in a serious tone of voice.

"From whom?"

"He didn't reveal his source," Lloyd replied.

"Maybe it's quite legitimate. I mean Ralph is the last kind of person who'd be associated with anything like this. He's squeaky clean," Max said.

"Maybe he gets off on the connection."

"What connection?" Max asked.

"One of your brother-in-law's clients is a wannabee pop singer called Lucy Hart."

"I've never heard of her," said Max.

"There's no reason why you should. She's new on the pop scene. Like a new-kid-on-the-block. She's had a couple of minor radio hits. She's bubbling under as they say."

"Who is she?" Max asked.

"She's Louis Delaney's daughter. That's probably how Colby knows him."

"What's this got to do with my missing sister?" Max asked.

"Maybe nothing," said Lloyd. "Or on the other hand it could be linked."

Max sat up. "How?" he asked.

"Use your imagination. Your sister goes missing. Maybe it's all tied in together."

"How?"

"Are the Lomax and Delaney people holding her, so Ralph does some dental work for their chums?"

Max was increasingly flummoxed. He couldn't get his head around this. He ruminated on his words for a few long moments. "Do the police know about this?" he asked.

"No idea," said Lloyd.

Max reflected for a moment and tried to get his thoughts together. "The police seem to think that Helena left Ralph because she's found a new man in her life," he said.

"What's the likelihood of that?" Lloyd asked.

"I honestly doubt it, but I don't know for sure," Max replied. "It might be genuine, or it could be a load of nonsense."

"An excuse to explain away her disappearance. Maybe?" Lloyd suggested.

"Maybe," replied Max. "What's Steve Chilton doing right now?" he asked.

"He's on the case. He's looking for her. Checking hotel listings. Plane manifests. Speaking to people. He's on the job."

"That's good. I trust he'll inform you as soon as he's got any firm information of her whereabouts," Max said.

"He will. One hundred per cent," Lloyd said, as if he felt it necessary to defend him.

There was a knock at the door. Lloyd got up and went to the door. "I'll see you shortly," he said.

"Thanks. I appreciate it," said Max.

"No problem," said Lloyd as he opened the door. Toby Bell, Max's personal assistant, was standing there. He had a file in his hand. Max invited him in. They chatted briefly about a rather large client acquisition, then Toby left him alone and closed the door behind him.

Max got up out of his chair. He stepped to the window and looked down on to the rooftops of the streets below, watching the traffic edging through the tight maze of city streets and thoroughfares and the swarm of people heading away from the City. He returned to his desk, turned his PC off and just sat back in his seat. He took a few moments to reflect on Lloyd's disclosure. The realisation that Ralph Colby knew some hardened villains and may have done work for them was frankly incredible, almost too bizarre for words, but it didn't mean to say it had anything to do with the disappearance of his sister.

Thursday 22nd June.

Over the course of the following day, Thursday, a senior executive team led by Petra DeVries and Sara Lynn interviewed Max's level of managers on a one-to-one basis. It was part of the redundancy consultation period, aligned to the drive to cut staff costs. In line with company policy he requested, without any obligation, a statement of the amount of money he would be awarded if he applied for and was granted voluntary redundancy. At forty-six years of age he might encounter a few problems securing a new post with another company at the same level of remuneration he currently enjoyed. His current earnings were in the region of three hundred thousand pounds a year before tax, plus profits from a company share scheme he had taken advantage of. Alternatively, he might walk into a new position with another firm at the same level of salary. A third alternative was to leave the financial sector all together and start a small business of his own. He had, for the past year or so, been thinking of starting a business buying and selling antiques. He had a good knowledge of antiques and how the market worked. His expertise was in furniture, especially French and Regency vintage.

Within hours of the meeting with Sara Lynn, Max was presented with a statement. The sum of money he could walk away with if he applied for voluntary redundancy, and it was approved, was: £1,960.000.

Friday 23rd June

The following day, Friday, was exactly two weeks since he had spoken to Ralph on the telephone. It was now over one month since Helena had vanished. At ten o'clock in the morning, there was a knock at the door. Lloyd Sherwood came into the office. He looked relaxed and calm, but then he always looked relaxed and calm no matter what. He seemed to possess a turn-off button which meant he never got tense or worked up about anything.

Lloyd was wearing a nice grey suit with a lemon silk tie at the neck of a white shirt. The rumour doing the rounds was that he had applied for voluntary redundancy, but the indications were that the company would turn down his request because he knew too much about the workings of the company for him to escape with all that knowledge.

He wasn't here to talk about that. He was here to talk about Max's missing sister. "I've spoken to Steve Chilton the private eye," he said. He liked saying *Private Eye*.

"I know who he is," said Max. "Remember I'm paying him a king's ransom."

Lloyd smiled. "He's got some information to share. Requested a one-to-one today."

"Where?" Max asked.

"Anywhere you want."

"What time?"

"Over lunch. Say about one,"

"Okay. Name the place."

"What about the path between St Paul's and the Millennium Bridge?" Lloyd said.

"Sounds as good as anywhere."

"I'll call him," said Lloyd, referring to Chilton. "One-fifteen on the path leading to the bridge."

Lloyd left the office and closed the door behind him.

The rest of that Friday morning was quiet, there wasn't a huge amount of buying and selling shares in the lead up to the weekend. It was getting on for ten to one when Lloyd returned.

Max informed Toby Bell that he was going out for a walk with Lloyd to get some fresh air. It was best not to tell him that he was having a clandestine meeting with a private detective. It would have been all around the office in ten minutes. Max wondered if Toby, who was young and keen, would get his job if he departed. Maybe not, Toby was a nice enough young man, but a lightweight. Still stranger things had happened.

# Chapter 7

Max and Lloyd walked the short distance towards St Paul's cathedral. The day was sunny but chilly. A stiff breeze was blowing in from the east. It's whistling edge vibrated against the side of the buildings in the tight packed streets. From St Paul's they crossed the road at Queen Victoria Street and walked down Peters Hill path that led onto Millennium Bridge. The walkway was busy with tourists and office workers on their lunchbreak. Some office workers were sitting on a wall eating a Chinese takeaway. Tourists were standing around a guy who was entertaining the crowd with his amazing sleight-of-hand playing-card illusion act. Two other entertainers, painted from top to bottom in gold paint, were posing as lifeless statues.

Max eyed the pretty office workers in their summer attire. That got him thinking thoughts about Rosetta. He wondered what she was doing now. Where she was? What she was wearing? Strange thoughts. She had a slim slender body. Nice legs. Her boobs were pert and succulent. Lloyd said something to him which he didn't catch, but it brought him out of the daydream and back to the here and now.

The pair of them ventured towards the edge of the river. The wind blowing downstream was taking the shine off the temperature. On the other side of the Thames was the brick wall and the cooling towers of the old power station that was now the Tate Modern building. Max glanced back to look at the dome of St Paul's dominating the gap between the buildings on either side of the walkway.

Lloyd indicated that he recognised the man standing by the metal rail, beside the start of the walkway that spanned the river.

Steve Chilton had his back to them but seemed to know they were about to arrive. He turned around to greet them. He was a man around forty years of age, wearing a checked jacket, shirt, no tie, casual slacks, and tan leather tasselled moccasins on his feet. He was a tall, lean fellow around six feet tall with jet black hair that looked as if it had been dyed, it was that black. He was holding a brown leather document holder in his left hand. A silver wristwatch on his right-hand wrist. Not a bad-looking man. He looked ex-military or police. He had that rigid posture and gait about him.

Lloyd greeted him. He introduced Max. "Max, this is Steve Chilton." Chilton nodded his head to him. Max held his hand out and they exchanged a handshake. He had a meaty clasp and a powerful grip.

"Shall we walk and talk?" Chilton asked.

"What across the bridge?" Lloyd asked.

"I was thinking more of the path along the side of the river," said Chilton, looking to Max.

"That's fine," said Max.

They immediately took off down a flight of six concrete steps to the tow-path running alongside a metal grill barrier that separated the path from the river below.

There were few people on the path. The stiff breeze seemed to have deterred some from walking. The wind was whipping up the surface of the river into gentle white tipped waves. Its colour was a lifeless, listless shade of mucky brown, though the sunlight was reflecting on the surface like twinkles of flashing diamonds. Max detected a faint aroma of salt.

A few yards ahead, was a vacant wooden bench, so they sat down and took in the scene. Chilton was inbetween Max and Sherwood. Lloyd had spread himself to deter anyone else from sitting down and disturbing them. They looked out across the river towards the roof of the Globe theatre on the South Bank and Southwark Bridge about one hundred yards downriver.

"I understand that you've been able to get some more information about my brother-in law, Ralph Colby-Lewis," Max said to Chilton.

Chilton looked ahead. "The information I've been able to obtain comes from an associate of a man called Louis Delaney. It suggests that your brother-in-law has in the past done some work for him," he said.

"What kind of work?" Max asked. "I know he has a client, Lucy Hart, or some such name."

"This work is nothing like that," said Chilton. "This work is re-arranging the teeth of people who have fallen out of favour with the gang."

"I'm not getting it," said Max.

"This is work without any injections. In a word he pulls out teeth when their owners don't want them removed. All without any prior numbing of the teeth and anaesthetic," Chilton said.

Max winced. "Oh my God. You're kidding me. Right?"

"No. That's what a reliable source told me."

"That's truly awful," said Max.

"It is if you're on the other end," said Chilton. "There's a chance your sister has been kidnapped by the gang or she left to get away from them on your brothers-in-law's say so."

"Geez," said Max. It was crazy. Almost unbelievable. He knew Colby may have had an edge to him, but this was totally bizarre and off-the-wall.

"That might account for the reason she hasn't told you, because she knows he's in deep with some villains," said Chilton.

"Why would Ralph agree to do that?" Max asked.

"Maybe he has little choice in the matter."

Max buttoned up his jacket. He was feeling a combination of the chill and a cold sensation from what Chilton was telling him.

"Maybe he had to do it for them," said the private detective.

"Why?"

"To pay off a debt of some kind."

"This is crazy," said Max. "I would have never put Colby down as someone who would ever consider doing something like this."

"You'd be surprised," said Chilton. "Some people you would never ever think could do horrible things, do horrible things. It's called being human."

"What can I do? I still need to know what has happened to Helena. Whether she's being held against her will."

"Or worse," said Chilton in a downbeat tone of voice. He moved his eyes from Max to watch a glass topped tourist boat glide down the river towards Tower Bridge. It was kicking up a deep swell that was slapping against the wall.

"Or worse," said Max repeating Chilton's line. "Like what?"

"She could be dead."

Max was stunned. He felt his heart drop and his world come crashing down. "No surely not," he said raising his voice.

"It's a possibility that you need to be aware of," said Chilton. They watched as Lloyd Sherwood suddenly stood up, took a few steps towards the barrier, put his hands on the top and looked over the edge to the dirty brown water twenty feet below.

"I need to go to the police with this," Max said, looking at Chilton.

"I would strongly advise that you don't do that."

"Why?" asked Max.

"Because if your sister is being held, it might put her in greater danger," he replied.

"I need to know what's become of her. I need to know for my own sanity," said Max, pleading his case.

"I can understand that. I've an idea that may be of use."

"What?" Max asked.

"I know someone by the name of Ingrid Prescott…"

"Ingrid who?" Max asked.

"Ingrid Prescott," he repeated.

"Who is she?"

"Ingrid Prescott is a psychic."

"A psychic!" said Max. "You can't be serious?"

"I'm very serious. I very rarely joke about such matters," he said stiffly.

"A clairvoyant. A soothsayer…" Max remarked.

"I prefer psychic phenomena myself," said Chilton. "She might be our only hope," he added.

"I don't believe this," said Max.

"Believe what?" Chilton asked.

"This," retorted Max.

"Please don't dismiss the idea out of hand," said Chilton. "It's a chance. It could be our only chance to discover what has happened to Helena. Because believe me I don't have a clue as to her whereabouts. I've contacted a lot of people I know and called in a few favours to try and find your sister, but the trail as gone as cold as the iceberg that sunk the Titanic."

Max looked at him. He could tell from his tone of voice and his expressive eyes that he was speaking from the heart. At least he had the balls to admit that he couldn't find her. As if to concur with this assessment a huge seagull landed on the top of the railing, directly opposite, raised its head skyward then let out a piecing shriek before flying off to join its compatriots on the metal cables attached to the Millennium Bridge.

Max was cold, confused and stunned. The revelation that Colby was an associate of a criminal gang, was like being told that Snow White was a nymphomaniac who had gone through the seven dwarfs. It was barmy. It didn't seem feasible in any way, shape or form.

"His connection with these criminals, what exactly is it?" he asked.

"What do you mean?" Chilton asked.

"How did they meet? Do you know?"

"Lucy Hart. She's Louis Delaney's daughter. She's on your brother-in-law's client list. I guess that's how he met Delaney."

"Where does this Delaney live?" Max asked.

"Out in Kent somewhere. Why?" Chilton asked.

"Just wondering," Max replied.

A group of three people, dressed like tourists, came wandering along the path and eyed the three men sitting on the bench. It looked a little odd that they were sitting together. Max waited until they had gone by. He took in a deep breath. He put his eyes on the glass and silver steel structure of the Shard. The sunlight was glinting in the upper panes of reflective glass. *Where is this heading*? he asked himself. Never in a million years would he have associated Ralph with anything so sordid. He didn't say anything for ten seconds, whilst he had a long think to himself. The chilly wind picking up off the water went straight through his jacket to leave his skin covered with goosepimples. He trembled with the cold.

"This psychic lady. The clairvoyant…" he said.

"Psychic phenomena," said Chilton.

"Okay. What does she do?" Max asked.

"She uses her power of preintimation to discover what has become of missing people," Chilton replied.

Max had no idea what he meant. "Is she successful?" he asked.

"Her success rate is well into the thirty percent bracket."

"Thirty percent! Is that good?" Max asked.

"Believe me. It's high."

"How do we go about beginning a search?"

"First, I arrange a meeting."

"Where?" Max asked.

"At a neutral venue, like a bookshop or someplace like that," Chilton said.

"What does she get out of it?" Max asked.

"Nothing. Her services are free of charge. You can pay her if you wish, but she might return any money you give her."

"Okay," said Max. "I don't suppose there's any harm in trying."

"Do you have a recent photograph of your sister she can have?" Chilton asked.

"Yes. I've got one."

"How old?"

"Just a couple of years. It's a black and white. Heads and shoulders. A kind of promotion photograph for her business."

"Perfect," said Chilton. "Bring it to the meeting."

"Anything else?" Max asked.

"No. I can't think of anything else for the moment."

"When can I meet…." asked Max forgetting her name.

"Ingrid Prescott," said Chilton.

"Ingrid Prescott," Max repeated.

He was dubious about using a psychic to help. He just didn't believe anyone he had never met before could have premonitions that might lead to finding his sister. He put it in the same category as hocus-pocus and witchcraft.

"I think she'll be able to meet you tomorrow. Is that okay?" Chilton asked.

"Yes. That's fine."

"If you want to give me your smart phone number. Or I'll give Lloyd a message to pass onto you. Your choice," Chilton said.

Max was put into a slight dilemma. He didn't want it to appear that he didn't trust Lloyd, but at the same time he wondered if it was better to seek to restrict his involvement. He thought about it for a few brief moments.

"Give it to Lloyd, if that's okay with you?" he said looking at his colleague.

"Fine," said Lloyd.

Chilton looked at Lloyd. "I'll call you soon. Confirm the time and venue," he said.

Lloyd said okay.

Chilton rose from the bench and stretched his legs, then he ran a hand over the small of his back, as if the bench boards had dug into his pelvis. He said a quick farewell, then departed and walked up the path, towards the steps leading up to the bridge with the document holder still in the tight grip of his hand.

Max looked at Lloyd and vice-versa. "Interesting guy," Max said. "Believes in psychics," he commented.

Lloyd nodded his head but didn't reply. He too had buttoned his jacket closed as the chilly breeze whipping off the Thames cut through him.

In the next moment they got off the bench and walked along the path. They walked back to the office building, mostly in silence, only stopping for a few moments to observe a busker on the street leading to St Paul's.

Max had to be careful. He didn't want too many people knowing about the supposed connection between Ralph Colby and a bunch of London criminals. It still hadn't really sunk in. He was pleased that he had met Chilton, face-to-face. At least he knew he was real and not a figment of Lloyd Sherwood's imagination.

# Chapter 8

When Max got into his office he requested that Toby Bell come in for a chat about a recent development in the market. It was the proposed takeover of a British car part supplier by a giant US conglomerate which was bound to push up its share value. After a brief five-minute meeting with Toby, he checked his PC for emails. There were two messages in his in-box. One was from Rosetta Sanchez. She asked him if they could meet next weekend as she would be coming home from Lisbon, but that wasn't until a week today. The second message was more interesting.

It was from DI Eileen Welsh. She informed him that the disappearance of Helena Colby would soon feature on the Metropolitan Police missing person web-page. Her name and details would be added to the list. It would appear on the site in the next day or two. He wondered what had prompted the police to move it onto the web-page. He asked himself if they had made a connection between Ralph Colby and the bunch of villains led by Louis Delany and Eric Lomax?

It still seemed incredibly absurd that Ralph Colby, the level headed, staid, highly esteemed orthodontist would be involved with a bunch of hardened gangster types, but he told himself that he shouldn't be really surprised by anything in this world.

Max wondered whether it would make sense to call DI Welsh to ask her if she knew of the link. Despite the advice from Chilton advising him not to he thought it was a good idea to do so. He picked up the telephone, however, before he could locate her telephone number in his contacts book, his smart phone pinged to tell him he had an incoming call. He hit the accept button. It was Lloyd Sherwood calling him.

Lloyd told him he had spoken to Chilton who had spoken to the psychic, Ingrid Prescott. She would be free to meet with him the next afternoon in a café at the back of a bookshop on Montchant Street in Bloomsbury at three o'clock. The bookshop was called, appropriately enough, '*The Bookworm*'.

Max asked Lloyd to call Chilton to tell him he would be there to meet with her. He ended the conversation with Lloyd, then wondered whether to call DI Welsh to tell her of the link to Louis Delaney, but decided against it, until he had spoken to Ms Prescott.


Saturday 24th June.

The following day was Saturday. Max had planned to go into the office for a couple of hours to work on a presentation he had to give to senior managers on Monday. Those one level up the pyramid to him, on the latest trends and performance on the market. As he had all the necessary data to hand he decided to work at home in peace and free from any distraction. Since he had put in a request for a statement of the pay-out he would receive if he went for and was accepted for voluntary redundancy, he found that he had lost a little

72

bit of motivation. Also, the situation with his missing sister didn't put him in a positive frame of mind.

He began to work on the presentation at nine o'clock. He did the first run-through at eleven, then worked on the second draft until midday, adding in a few extra bar graphs and pie-charts. The senior executives loved to see a pie-chart.

Outside the day was sunny and pleasantly warm. The chill breeze of yesterday had dropped and the light pressing at the window gave the room a nice summer glow.

The presentation was complete by one o'clock. He saved it to a file, which he emailed to Toby. He asked him to save it to his file, print off a dozen copies and have them bound with a hard back and a clear Perspex front sheet, and have them on his desk for Monday morning so he could take them into the meeting in the afternoon.

It was two o'clock when he left his flat in Swiss Cottage. He had remembered to take the picture frame that contained a black and white photograph of Helena, that he had on the top of a sideboard. He placed the frame into a document holder. It was just a head and shoulders picture, taken the previous year or so, of her smiling at the camera for a marketing campaign. Helena wasn't a ravishing beauty, but neither was she ugly. She was Helena, his kith and kin. When he thought about that, it almost moved him to tears.

Then it hit him hard square between the eyes and he found himself going down memory lane. In the next instant he recalled scenes from summer holidays he had spent with his parents and Helena. Their parents would take them to places like Scarborough and Whitby and other small seaside resorts on the east coast of northern England. Max's father, Gerald, was born up there so he felt that he had to take his children to the places he had been too when he was a kid. At the time the holidays had been horrendous, but now looking back he was quite nostalgic for those times. He and Helena would play on the beach, then search in rock pools for star fish, using the nets their father had bought them from a beach side stall. Then if they got lucky he would take them on a Ferris wheel or on the dodgem cars in a nearby fun-fair. Or if it was raining they would go into the amusements, put a ten pence piece in a slot machine and try to hook a cuddly toy by using a kind of mechanical hook to grab a prize.

Then there were the camping holidays in the New Forest, when their father would put up two big tents on a camping site. Helena and he would share one. Their parents would be in the other. Their mother would cook some food on a gas stove and they would sit around a fold-up table, eating beans and sausages. Then at night they would all sleep under the stars. As the years passed the memories faded, but Max did often think about those times and right now, that his sister was missing, all those memories came flooding back. They brought back so many happy moments. He hoped that one day soon he would be able to speak to his sister and go back down memory lane.


'The Bookworm' bookshop and café was on Montchant street in the heart of Bloomsbury. It wasn't a very big place. It was crammed into a tight space between a Greek food store on one side, and a Tesco Express, on the other. It was an independent book store with an emphasis on small publishers' output and new authors. Judging by the window display, a kind of melting pot of new-age material meets the twenty-first century.

Max entered. There was no one inside browsing the shelves at three on a Saturday afternoon, which came as a surprise. The first thing he was aware of was the aroma of the books set out along rows of timber shelving. The floor was plain wood planks that had been sanded and painted over with a hard lacquer varnish. Pale green walls blended into the new-age theme and big leaved potted plants were dotted here and there. There was a counter at which a guy with long stringy hair, a scruffy goatee beard and John Lennon style glasses was standing reading a pamphlet.

He looked up and greeted Max with a nod of the head, then carried on what he was doing. Beyond the counter, towards the back, was a space occupied by two low-level, black leather sofas set in front of a low table. Beyond that was a tiny café area of no more than three small metal round tables, each covered by a shiny plastic cover. Placed against the back wall was a glass cabinet full of slices of cakes, pasties, and chocolate brownies. A self-service coffee machine was gurgling away on a table underneath a staircase going up to the first floor.

A lady was sitting at one of the tables. She had her head down, looking at a paperback book on the table. As Max came closer, she raised her head and looked at him.

She looked at be around his own age, maybe a couple of years younger. More around Helena's age. She had long copper-red hair that snaked down past her shoulders. She was wearing a white jacket with wide lapels, over a turquoise blouse. A mug containing a hot beverage was on the table, along with a plate that held a slice of half-consumed rice cake.

Her eyes stayed on his for a moment, then she gave him a smile from a face that contained soft features, clear blue eyes, a slender nose, and thin lips. The image of a psychic he had created in his mind was stereotypically of someone middle aged, frumpy looking with wild hair, maybe a touch eccentric. She wasn't like that at all. Quite the contrary. She had the merest hint of blusher on her cheeks and blue eyeliner. On each of her index and small fingers she wore a stone-centred gold band ring. There was a big hessian tote bag at her side. She was wearing brown corduroy pants that had flared cuffs at her feet.

He stepped close to her. "You must be... Ingrid?" he asked in an enquiring tone. Just in case she wasn't.

"And you must be Max Deardon."

"Yes." He held his hand out.

"Nice to meet you."

She took his hand and they exchanged a very brief handshake. Her hand was long and slender and bony to the touch. Her skin was as smooth as silk. He placed the document holder down and rested it against the legs of a chair.

"Do you want a refill?" he asked, thrusting his chin at the half empty coffee cup in front of her.

"No thanks," she said. "I'm nearly done."

"I'll just help myself. Who do I pay?" he asked.

"Pay Paul at the counter," she said. "As you leave."

"Okay."

She obviously knew the chap with the long hair and the straggly goatee at the counter. Max went to the coffee machine, took a white mug, and helped himself to a plain black coffee from the machine.

He put the mug on a saucer, then came back to the table and sat a couple of feet across the table from her. Over the sound system, at very low volume, a string orchestra classical piece of music was floating out of a speaker attached to the underside of the staircase. He had heard the piece before but didn't recognise the composer.

She took the mug in front of her in her long-tapered fingers and put it to her lips but didn't take a sip. She settled her blue-green eyes on his.

"I understand that you're looking for your sister," she said in a low voice. She had the merest hint of a West Country accent.

"That's correct."

"Can you give me the background?" she asked.

"Sure. Absolutely," he said after a momentary pause whilst he took in her features. He reached to a side, took the document holder, unzipped it and withdrew the frame containing the photograph of his sister. "This is my sister Helena. She's aged forty-three."

He put the frame on the table, facing her the right way around so she could see it. "She's been missing for more than a month," he said.

Ingrid took a sip from the mug. She held it not by the handle but clamped in the fingertips of each hand. She didn't say anything, so he continued. "My brother-in-law, Ralph Colby, Colby-Lewis to give him his full name, contacted me to say she had left their home following an argument."

As he spoke she fleetingly dropped her eyes to look at the photograph of the half-smiling Helena.

"Tell me more," she encouraged.

"There's not a great deal more to tell."

"Does she have any children?"

"No."

"What, if anything, does your sister do for a living?"

"She's a high-flying business consultant. She works for several companies around the world." Ingrid didn't bat an eyelid. She continued to gaze at the photograph.

Max continued the introduction. "They've been married for fifteen years. In all that time, I've never detected that their marriage has been in any kind of trouble."

"What does her husband do?" she asked.

"He's an orthodontist, with a practice on Harley Street," he replied.

Just then the door to the store opened. Max glanced back to see an elderly couple enter. They engaged in conversation with Paul, the chap at the counter.

"Tell me about your parents."

"Both deceased. Six years ago," he said.

"Did you have good parents?" she asked.

"Yeah, I'd say so," he replied after a moment. "Why do you ask?"

"I'm just trying to get a feel of her character," she said.

"Are you close?" she asked.

"Yes. I think you'd say so."

She put the rim of the cup to her lips. "You think she may have come to some harm?" she asked, then she took a sip of the coffee in the mug.

"It's possible," he replied.

"Why?"

He told her about what Steve Chilton had said about Ralph Colby's supposed connection to some villains. He revealed that he had spoken to a DI Welsh who told him that Colby had said that she had left him to take up with another man. Ingrid asked him where they lived. He replied that they had a home in the Berkshire countryside and a flat in the Barbican.

"I will need to be taken to the house," she said.

"Which one?" he asked.

"The one in Berkshire."

"Why?"

"Because, if I'm going to be able to find her. I'll need to be close to or in the house to feel her spirit."

"What do you mean?" he asked. "Actually, in the house?"

"Yes."

"Is that necessary?"

"Yes. I'm not picking up anything untoward just looking at the photograph. There's no feeling of any connection nor is there any premonition of hurt. I will have to get into the house to feel something that might lead me to knowing where she is now," she said.

"Okay." Max was beginning to think that this could be a lot more complex than he anticipated.

She put her deep, green-blue, eyes on his and looked at him as if she was trying to read his mind, through some telepathic channel. Her eyes had a magnetic quality that could draw you in. Her skin was as smooth as porcelain and without any blemishes what-so-ever.

"I see a sincerity in her face," she said. "I'm not feeling any strong emotions of trauma or anything like that. I feel she is at peace. That she is still alive and well."

"That's good news," he said, encouraged by her words.

Ingrid Prescott said nothing. She sat into the round back of the chair. From behind Max the till sounded. The assistant had made a sale. Max glanced back to see the elderly couple stepping out of the door. The lady was clutching a plastic bag containing a purchase. He turned back to face Ingrid Prescott.

"What do we do next?" he asked.

"I'll need to get into the house to see if I can pick up any feelings." She reiterated.

"I'll have to think of a way of been able to do that. It might be a lot easier said than done," he warned.

She reached down, raked into her tote bag, and pulled out a purse like container. She opened it and extracted a business card.

"My telephone number is on my card. Give me a call. May I take the picture frame?" she asked.

"Of course," he said as he took the card out of her hand.

She glanced at the narrow wrist watch on her right hand. "I must be going now," she announced. "I'll wait for you to call me. It was nice to make your acquaintance," she said. She stood up and extended her long slim legs. She was slender and as tall as him, at around five feet nine and, he noticed, her shoes had flat soles.

She took hold of the picture frame and slipped it inside her bag. Then she was gone. He watched her walk to the counter and pay the chap for the beverage she had drunk. She had not finished the rice cake. He had not touched his coffee either. He glanced at the card she had given him. It had both a landline and mobile telephone number on it, along with a web address.

Max left the bookshop a few minutes later, paying for the coffee he hadn't drunk. He returned home to Swiss Cottage.

# Chapter 9

Monday 26<sup>th</sup> June

The weekend didn't last long enough. It was soon the first day of the working week again. When he got into his office, on Monday morning, Max found the twelve bound reports he required for the days meeting on his desk. He took one and flicked through it. It looked okay. All the presentation slides were in the correct order and there was a lined sheet at the back for notes, should any member of the senior management team care to make any. He put the pile of reports to one side, then took his telephone and called Lloyd Sherwood. He asked him if he would be so kind as to pop into his office. Lloyd said no problem he would be there in a couple of minutes.

Max got up from the desk, stepped to the window and watched the commuters and the office workers heading to their place of employment. All scurrying along to earn a crust. All human life was down there, he thought.

Lloyd came into his office a couple of minutes after being summoned. He looked well-presented as always. His tie was tight into the collar of his shirt. He checked it was straight then he ran a hand over his recently shaved head. He came to the window to join Max and looked down onto the stream of people heading along the streets below.

"How did the meeting with Ingrid Prescott go?" he asked.

"All right. She's an interesting lady. Quite nice looking if the truth be told," he said with a wink.

"That's a positive then," said Lloyd smirking. "Did she come up with any leads?"

"Not really. She wants to get into their Berkshire house. But I for the life of me don't know how I'm going to achieve that. I've been thinking about it all the flaming weekend. I reckon Ralph might be pissed-off at me for getting the police involved without telling him. He'll have the hump. I must find a way of getting Ingrid into the house to see if she can pick up any vibes."

Lloyd quickly realised that Max was hoping that he would come up with an idea. He thought about it. Silence descended in the office, while the noise from the trading floor was just as frenetic as usual.

"Maybe there is a way," Lloyd said after a few moments.

"How?" Max asked.

"Simple. Visit your bother-in-law at home," he said. "Take Ingrid with you. Tell him she's your latest muse."

Max sucked on his teeth. "I'm not sure that will work," he said. "But why didn't I think of that?"

"No harm in trying," said Lloyd. "What makes you think it won't work?"

"It's Ralph. He might be angry with me for the reasons I've already mentioned."

"Tell him you've come to apologise. He might buy it."

"He might," agreed Max. "You know it's not such a bad idea. He's got a bit of an ego when it comes to me. It will appeal to his sense of importance. He has in the past sought to belittle me. Here's another chance," he said.

"Well, here's your opportunity," said Lloyd. "Take him a peace offering. What does he like?"

"Expensive wine and fine claret," he replied.

"There you are. Buy him an expensive bottle of wine. Use it as a peace offering. Introduce Ingrid to him as your new girlfriend. He might just go for it."

"Okay. Good idea," Max said. He was now convinced.

The conversation ended when there was a knock at the door. It was Toby Bell. He greeted his boss and Sherwood. Max thanked him for getting the reports together. Max liked Toby at lot. Maybe Toby assumed he would get his job if he left the firm. Max had told Sara Lynn, that in his opinion, Toby wasn't ready to step into his shoes, not just yet.

Lloyd left the office with Toby, leaving Max to get on with his day. He turned his PC on and checked his private 'Hotmail' account. There was another message from DI Welsh to tell him the bulletin on the Met's missing person web-page had gone live. He immediately logged onto the site and checked it out.

Sure enough, it was on the missing person page. Just another name on a list of thirty, or so, names. It said.

*Missing from her home in Berkshire and the Barbican district of London. Helena Colby-Lewis, Helena Colby. Age 43. Five feet five tall. Medium build. Light brown hair.*

*If you have seen Helena, please call the Missing Person unit at Theobald's Street Station in Holborn or at the Central Police station in Reading,*

It gave a long telephone number next to a recent photograph of Helena that Ralph must have supplied to the police.

Max took his telephone and called Ralph's mobile phone number. There was no response after a dozen calls so he aborted the call before it went to voice mail.

That evening he left the office at six-thirty. He arrived home one hour later. There was one missed call on his landline. He recognised the number as that of the Colby's Berkshire home. Colby must have been at home in the house. That was unusual because he tended to spend Monday, Tuesday, and Wednesday at his flat in the Barbican.

Max quickly redialled the number. Colby answered it on the third ring. He sounded in good spirits. He asked Max why he had called him. Max had to pause for a moment to collect his thoughts.

"I see the police have issued a missing person bulletin for Helena," he said.

"I know. I've seen it on-line."

"That's good then," said Max.

"Of course, it is," said Colby.

There was a moment of silence, rather like a pregnant pause. "Is that all?" Colby asked.

"Yeah. No. I mean. I just wanted to call you to say I'm sorry for going to the police first and not tell you." Colby didn't reply. Perhaps he was searching for an appropriate response. Although he couldn't see him Max could almost see the sneer on his face.

"What if I come to see you one day soon. I'll bring a good bottle of wine with me," said Max.

"I'm not sure if that's a good idea," said Colby.

"Why not?" Max asked.

"I'm relaxing this week. I've closed the studio for the week unless I get an emergency referral or an important client calls," he said. "I'm at home all week."

That would account for why he was home in Berkshire, thought Max. He had an idea. "I'll introduce you to my new girlfriend," he said.

"Err," said Colby to himself as he ruminated for a few long moments over what Max had just said.

"All right," said Colby. "You can come on Wednesday. Make it about three. I see there's life in the dog then," he said and chuckled to himself.

"Certainly is," said Max.

"What's her name?" he asked.

"Ingrid."

"What happened to what's-her-face. Rosetta?"

"Back home in Lisbon. I don't see her anymore," Max said, lying.

Colby decided to cut the conversation short as it suddenly occurred to him that it was inappropriate to be discussing women when his own wife had left him. He quickly said goodbye and see you on Wednesday.

Max terminated the call. He looked at the telephone for a few short moments, wondering if Colby had detected the slight hesitance in his voice. Did he suspect that the new girlfriend story was a load of rubbish? Did he know of a psychic called Ingrid Prescott?

Unlikely. Colby wasn't the kind of person who went in for soothsayers, or the paranormal, or anything remotely like that. He maybe wouldn't suspect a thing.

Max waited for a further five minutes to see if Colby would call him back. He didn't, so he called Ingrid to put her in the picture. They talked for less than a couple of minutes. She wasn't convinced that the idea of her posing as his new love interest had any mileage, but she seemed content to go along with it. He said he would pick her up from outside the book store in Bloomsbury at one-fifteen on Wednesday. She said okay.

# Chapter 10

At two in the afternoon the senior executives and the senior management team met in the boardroom for the third quarter projection meeting. Max handed out the presentation packs, then he went to the front of the room to present his predictions for the months of July, August, and September. The third quarter was usually the quietest period of the year as investors and large fund managers didn't do a great deal of business in these months.

After the meeting, which lasted for forty minutes, several colleagues met for an informal chat about the future of the firm. Several of his close colleagues told Max that they had applied for the voluntary redundancy package. It seemed as if the firm was seeking to ditch a number of those on big salaries, then to promote from within, but not at such high remuneration packages. Or in other words, cut costs, but still attempt to maintain the same level of service and expertise as they had now, but on less expenditure. A difficult juggling act for any firm in such a high-stakes business. The firm relied on a small team of analysts to predict movements in the market before they occurred. A good analyst using a combination of logarithms and other calculus could predict movements to a 95% level of accuracy. But it took a long period of time for an analyst, like Max Deardon, to collect all the requisite skills. Getting rid of all those in the £300,000 a year salary bracket would reduce costs, but not necessarily make the company any more profitable. Not his problem, concluded Max. He had been thinking seriously about purchasing the antique business he had seen advertised in a local North London newspaper.

During the afternoon, Max received an email from Sara Lynn, Head of Personnel, in the London office. She told him that his application for voluntary redundancy was going to be considered by a panel headed by Chief Executive, Petra DeVries and several senior executives on Thursday afternoon. He would receive confirmation of their decision the following day.

If he was being truthful, he was somewhat ambivalent about the whole process. He was getting to that stage of his working life where he couldn't care less. It was as if they were trying to suck the fight out of his body. Nonetheless, he emailed Sara to say thanks for the update. Later, at around four, he left the office for thirty minutes to visit a wine store on Cheapside to purchase a bottle of Bordeaux Claret at a price of one hundred and eighty-five pounds, a bottle.

On his return he opened a new email from Rosetta Sanchez to remind him that she would be home on Friday afternoon and to ask him if he planned to take her out for the evening. He replied inviting her to come to his home and yes, of course, he would take her out to dinner on Friday evening. He didn't want to tell her about Helena, she would only ask more questions and complicate matters, so he kept quiet on that account.

He took a moment to have a breather and to think about everything that was going on in his life at the moment. He was going through a tumultuous period. He had, not only the disappearance of his sister to think about, but the possibility that he wouldn't have a job this time next week, though the severance package did ensure that losing his job wouldn't cause him endless sleepless nights. But also, that Rosetta was coming back into his thoughts. At forty-six years of age he found that his life was passing by so quickly. Perhaps he needed something else to do to recharge his batteries. If he was going into the antiques business, he had to do it before Father Time made it not worth pursuing. And if he was going to ask Rosetta to move in with him, he had better do it soon.


Tuesday 27th June

Tuesday came around. The sun which had baked London for the last few days didn't let up. It was horizon to horizon blue skies over the city and across much of the south of England. He spent the evening pottering about in his flat, tidying up and making it presentable for Rosetta when she came on Friday.

By late evening he had cleaned the flat and got around to changing the bed sheets. At nine o'clock he visited a local supermarket to stock up on food. The life of a bachelor sometimes didn't always appeal to him, but overall, he was quite content.

It had been eighteen days since Ralph had contacted him to tell him his sister had left their home in Berkshire following an argument. No matter what he just couldn't get over the fact that she hadn't contacted him to tell him she was okay. Which led him to believe, no matter what Ingrid Prescott said, that she was either in some kind of sticky situation or perhaps even dead. He was still finding it hard to believe that Ralph Colby was involved with some underworld criminal types. It just didn't seem plausible, but maybe it was true.

# Chapter 11

Max had booked Wednesday off work as annual leave. It was quarter to one when he left home. He drove his Audi Quattro soft top convertible, the short distance into central London and into Bloomsbury. He kept the top up. He didn't want Ingrid Prescott to think he was some aging Lothario who used a smart car to try and impress ladies. It was another nice day. The temperature was reaching its zenith, then it would begin to get slightly cooler and showery for the start of the Wimbledon fortnight, which began on Monday.

He arrived in front of the bookstore on Montmatch Street a few minutes ahead of schedule. Despite being a decent day there were few people about on the pavements. He parked close to the front of the 'Bookworm' and waited for Ingrid to arrive.

It was another few minutes before she appeared on the pavement. She was dressed in a different summer jacket and a maxi skirt, with black ankle boots on her feet. He liked her dress sense. Elegant and stylish. She had pulled her hair back and tied it using a scrunchy so more of her long slender face and jaw line were visible. She resembled an actress he had once seen in some early Clooney pot-boiler of a movie but didn't know her name. Max was impressed. Colby would be impressed that he had managed to pull such a nice looking lady. The expensive bottle of Claret he had bought for his brother-in-law was on the back seat in its presentation box.

She stepped to the front of the store which was open but didn't go inside. Max got out of his car, walked the few yards along the pavement until she saw him and came to meet him. Max took off the shades over his eyes and placed them into his jacket pocket.

She had a different shoulder bag around her right shoulder to the hessian tote bag. This was more lady-about-town. He turned, walked her to his car and opened the front passenger door for her. She graciously slid into the seat. The seat was too close to the dashboard, so she had to release the lock and push the seat back, in order that she could fit her legs into the footwell. Once she was settled, he went around the front, opened the driver's door, and got in.

He got the motor running, pulled out of the tight space, and set the car going ahead towards the junction with Euston Road. The traffic was okay, nothing too overbearing.

They didn't say much. Hardly a word to each other. She seemed in a reflective mood. Perhaps wondering if the boyfriend-girlfriend ruse would work. His brother-in-law might be taken in by the couple who did look well matched, although they would lack that spark of affection that new lovers often display.

Within a matter of thirty minutes of leaving Bloomsbury, the Audi was on the M4 and approaching the first turn off for Heathrow Airport. They had indulged in some chat about what they were going to do once they arrived in the house. The plan was for him to introduce her to Ralph, Ingrid to comment about the size of the house, then Max to ask Ralph to give them a tour of the house and the back garden.

They agreed on a back story in case Colby should ask them where they had met. They had met in the bookstore in Bloomsbury several weeks ago and had chatted, over coffee, about their favourite book. His was 'The Magus' by John Fowles, Ingrid's was 'To Kill a Mockingbird' by Harper Lee. Then he had asked her to join him for dinner that evening. She had agreed, and it led to them becoming acquainted. It did sound a little far-fetched, a tad screwball, but hopefully it would work. If Colby mentioned Rosetta Sanchez, then she was to tell him that she knew about her, which might convince him that they had talked and were on the same page.

After zooming along the M4 for twenty miles they reached the first turn for Reading. He took the slip-road off, went around a roundabout, under the motorway to a second roundabout where he took the third exit to skirt around the eastern outskirts of the town. They were soon out into the pleasant leafy countryside. The day was pleasant and warm. The sky was a combination of paint-ball white, fluffy clouds in an aqua blue sky.

They passed through the first village, called Elson, then a mile further on into a hamlet of a dozen roadside homes, several with thatched roofs and loads of 'Old English' character. The countryside had become hilly with rolling fields and vistas to the flat plains of the low-lying countryside to the east. After going through the hamlet, they passed a junction with a road on the right that went down a steep hillside, to a wooden copse just beyond, then the picturesque village of Abbotsford. The Colby house was situated in its own parcel of land on the sweep of a sharp right-left dog-leg in the road.

After driving for another two hundred yards or so the house came into view on the right-hand side of the road. It was a large property with a mock Tudor front and a high, steeple roof. There was a low bramble hedge in front of a six-foot-high brick wall at the other side of a grass verge that separated the road from the property. The wall ran down both sides of the house. Max knew from previous visits that, at the back, there were a line of tall poplar trees that formed the boundary.

Max came to the first of two iron gates. He swung the car off the road, went through the open gate and onto a pebble stone forecourt in front of the house. A BMW seven series car with a 2017 plate was parked on the forecourt in front of the porched entrance to the house.

He parked parallel to the BMW and came to a halt. The Colby house was around thirty years old. It was one of those out of the way single developments for wealthy owners wanting a place of isolation in rolling countryside, but near enough to a thriving town with excellent transport links to get to and from London in little time. The façade was red brick with black and white horizontal stripes between the bedroom windows and the eves.

Helena and Ralph Colby had lived here for the past ten years. Max had been here on several occasions in that time, but only once or twice in the past couple of years. The last time was about a year ago to attend the grand opening of the fifteen-metre swimming pool at the rear of the house.

The sound of the wheels on the stones alerted Colby to their arrival. The front door opened, and he appeared under the shade of the porch roof. He was dressed casually in an open blue shirt over a grey sport vest. He was wearing knee length baggy shorts and had flip-flops on his feet.

His eyes went straight to Ingrid as she uncurled her long legs to climb out of the tight confines of the car. According to Helena, Ralph had developed a bit of a roving eye over the past couple of years, but he had remained faithful and married to her. She said that his bark was worse than his bite.

He smiled towards Max and raised his hand. "Welcome to my abode," he said in a hearty type of way.

Max took the box containing the bottle of Claret off the back seat and climbed out of the car. He came next to Ingrid, took her by the turn of her elbow and they stepped towards the entrance.

"Ralph, may I introduce you to Ingrid?" he said. Remembering not to reveal her surname.

"Delighted," said Colby with a grin on his face.

"Ingrid, this is my brother-in-law, Ralph Colby."

Colby's grin turned into a smile. "Welcome," he said. Then he led them through the front door and along a hallway which opened out into a wide square shaped central reception area. There was a staircase to the left and a passageway straight ahead that led to a door which opened onto the back of the house. The ground floor had five rooms: a spacious kitchen, Colby's study, a sport room, a room he called the 'drawing room' and finally a large sitting room that looked out onto the back of the house. The garden was at least fifty yards long and wide. The shield of tall, tightly packed trees at the perimeter provided an effective screen. Beyond the trees was the beginning of a rolling hillside that led to a tree lined copse about five hundred yards away.

Colby took them across the reception area and into the sitting room. It was furnished in a neutral style with fine furniture and decorations, but it wasn't over the top. A plain cream carpet covered the floor.

The room was dominated by a semi-circular six-seater sofa that was covered with mink-coloured throws. There was a gold-frame mirror above the open fireplace. French windows opened onto a brick patio and the area around the swimming pool.

"Here's a gift for you," Max said as he handed Colby the case containing the bottle of Claret.

Colby slid the lid open, lifted the bottle out and examined the label. "Very nice. Thank you. I'll enjoy drinking that," he said. "Take a seat," he encouraged, looking to the sofa. "I'll put it in my booze collection in the kitchen," he said, referring to the Claret.

Max looked to Ingrid and they shared a face that said so far so good. They sat on the sofa with a narrow gap between them. Light was pouring in through the French windows.

She immediately crossed her legs. She was calm and collected. Then she closed her eyes and shivered as if a sudden cold shower had come over her.

"You okay?" Max asked in a whisper.

"I'm feeling an intense coldness," she said. "The air is heavy with a sense of dread," she added.

"Like what?" he asked.

"Something bad happened in this house. Something very troubling," she said. Her eyes were tightly closed, and her mouth was clamped. She must have been having a paranormal episode.

Just then Colby called out from the kitchen. "Can I get you anything to drink," he asked. Moments later he came back into the room.

"Not for me," said Max.

"Ingrid?" Colby asked.

She had opened her eyes and her face was back to normal. The episode must have passed. She shook her head. "Not for me," she said.

Colby advanced towards the French windows, then stopped and turned to face them.

"So, what brings you here?" he asked his brother-in-law.

"I felt a little guilty about going to the police before you," Max explained.

Colby's face remained fixed in a nondescript expression. "I can understand your action," he said. "I didn't want to tell you the real reason why Helena left me. Call it shame if you want to. I didn't want to appear depressed."

"I can understand that," Max said. Almost repeating word for word what Colby had said.

"Where did you two meet?" Colby suddenly enquired.

Max told him that they had met in a bookstore in Bloomsbury. Colby seemed to take it at face value. He looked at Ingrid. "Are you feeling okay?" he asked.

Max glanced at Ingrid to see that her brow was peppered with beads of perspiration. "Can I have a glass of water please," she asked. "I'm feeling a little flush."

"Of course," said Colby. He went across the room. Max watched him go out of the door. He waited for a moment, then turned to Ingrid.

"Are you okay?" he whispered.

"I'm not feeling well. I'm having a premonition of the presence of death in this house," she said. She visibly quivered.

"You are sure?" he asked.

"I can feel it in my heart," she said. "I can see the face of a woman and a man and see an image of death," she said.

In the next moment, Colby came back into the room with a beaker of water in his hand. "It's bottled water. Not tap," he said. He placed the glass in her outstretched hand. She put it to her lips and took a long sip.

"Are you sure you're okay?" he asked with a genuine tone of concern in his voice.

"Sorry," said Ingrid. She suddenly, unexpectedly, got to her feet and headed straight out of the sitting room, followed by Max, then Colby.

By the time Colby got into the reception area they were at the door and stepping out under the shade of the porch. It was so sudden it had taken Max by surprise. He turned to look at Colby. "I'm really sorry Ralph. We've got to go. Ingrid is not feeling well. I'll be in touch," he said.

The sudden turn of events clearly stunned Colby. It was most bizarre. He looked extremely puzzled by their swift departure.

Ingrid went around the back of the car and got into the passenger seat, Max got into the driver's seat. He started the car and drove across the pebbles, out of the open gate and turned left onto the road.

"Are you okay?" he asked. She was breathing heavily and drawing in breaths with a panting sound.

"There's a death-spirit in that house," she repeated. "I had a vision of a woman being killed and a man struggling," she said.

"Was the woman Helena?" he asked.

"I didn't see her face in my vision," she replied.

"Who was it?"

"Someone younger than your sister."

Max said nothing. He was on the road leading into the hamlet of cottages and the village of Elson. They were just coming to the single road on the left that led down the steep hill to a wooded copse at the bottom of the descent. As he neared the junction Ingrid reached out and grabbed his left arm.

"Turn here," she instructed.

"It's straight on," he said.

"No. Turn left here," she demanded tersely.

He put the anchors on and swung the Audi into the left turn. She let go of his arm. A black and white sign on the verge side said: 'Abbotsford 2'

The road was just wide enough for two vehicles to pass side-by-side at low speed. It dropped down a steep decline for a quarter of a mile or so towards a wooded area at the bottom where the road levelled out.

She went into one of her premonition episodes. "Are you having a vision?" he asked. She didn't reply. She seemed to be on another journey. The one inside her head. Max felt uneasy.

He headed down to the bottom of the long steep descent. As it came level to the beginning of a wooded copse on the left she let out a shriek that stunned Max. He jammed on the brakes and reduced speed from forty to five miles an hour in a heartbeat.

"Good God. What?" he asked.

She didn't respond. She had her head back and her eyes tightly closed. He looked into the wooded copse. He moved on for another forty to fifty yards then came level to a metal gate. Beyond the gate were rows of tall, thin pine trees then an open area, then more rows of trees, perhaps forty to fifty wide. The afternoon sunlight was cascading into the wood, casting shade through the treetops, so the light was speckled.

"I'll stop here," he said.

He pulled up in a dry mud space in front of the gate. A padlock and chain secured the gate to an adjoining post. A beaten earth track from the gate led through the trees into the open area.

Ingrid came out of the premonition and back to the here and now. She said, nothing, but got out of the car and stepped towards the gate. She squeezed through a gap between the post and the gate and stepped onto the track and into the wooded area.

Max got out of the car. He followed her, forced himself through the gap and followed her up the track, keeping about five yards behind her. Her feet made little sound on the grass. A breeze suddenly got up to gently rustle the tops of the tall, thin pine trees. A carrion crow emerged from out of a nest and flew off, making a screeching sound. The aroma of the grass and earth filled his nostrils.

After walking along the path for around thirty yards, she advanced into the open area, then stopped and slowly turned three hundred and sixty degrees. Max caught up with her. She turned to look at him. Her eyes went up to the sky.

'Here' she said, saying just that one word.

"What's here?" he asked.

"A death-presence," she said.

Max looked at the thick grassland. It was nothing more than a wide patch of earth with grass growing to a height of six inches or so. There was nothing obvious to indicate that any shallow graves or anything remotely like that were here.

On one side to the left, beyond the trees, was the steep rise that led up the hill to the back of the Colby home. Due to the distance and the steepness of the hill it wasn't possible to see the house, not even the roof.

Max elected to say nothing. If she had a premonition that something had happened in this copse, then he had no reason to doubt that she had genuine reason to believe it. He stepped a couple of yards to her side. At this spot the earth felt spongy and moist. She moved away from him and began to walk around in narrow circles.

He waited for a few moments, then he decided to do something. He set off along the path, out of the open area, and back along the track to the gate. Once there he squeezed through the gap.

He got into his car, found his mobile phone, then the card DI Welsh had given him. He tapped the number into his phone, but the strength of the signal was so poor it wouldn't connect. Out here in the sticks, several miles from any great urban build-up there wasn't an adequate communication mast. He could do nothing for the time being, but to return into the wooded area and go back to Ingrid.

She was still wandering around in circular movements. She looked as if she was in a trance. Though, as he appeared, she stopped and looked at him.

"There's definitely a presence here," she said.

"What do you feel?" he asked.

"I have a great sense of foreboding. A death presence," she repeated, not for the first time.

"Can you be more specific?" he asked.

"There are dead bodies buried here in this area," she said.

He instantly noticed the reference to more than one. "Bodies?" he asked.

"Several," she said.

He looked through the line of tall trees all set in a managed formation up the incline towards the back of the Colby house. It occurred to him that if there had been a murder in the house, whoever had committed it could have dragged a body down the hill and brought it here for burial in a shallow grave. It was well out of sight from the road, which was hardly used. The site was secluded.

"I think we'd better report your premonition to the police," he said.

She didn't respond.

"I can't get a signal on my phone. I know there's a village a couple of miles down the road." He looked to his car. "Let's go there and try to use a telephone."

"All right," she said.

They moved away from the open area, back along the path and onto the car.

# Chapter 12

The next village, Abbotsford, was around two miles along the road. Despite the road being narrow and winding, they were there in less than six minutes. The time was getting on for four o'clock. The antique store Max had once visited might be open on a Wednesday.

He drove by the village church. There were a few houses in the village, a pub, a takeaway, and an ice cream parlour. There were few people about. The antique store was on a corner. It was a ramshackle building that had once been an old garage, cum petrol station. It still had the original corrugated roof. A couple of cars were parked outside so he put his car next to them. He killed the engine, got out and stepped to the door. Ingrid choose to remain in the car.

He went inside. It hadn't changed much from the last time he had been in here. There was an aisle sandwiched between the displays of old china, pictures, jewellery, crockery, paintings, and general bric-a-brac. An authentic, colourful, tin advertising board for Capstan Full-Strength cigarettes caught his eye.

The lady who must have been the owner-manager was standing behind a counter, surrounded by pots and various other bone-china objects in a glass cabinet. She greeted him with a smile. "Please. Do you have a telephone I can use?" he asked.

She looked at him.

"I have an emergency. My smart phone can't pick up a signal."

She continued to look at him as if the words 'smart phone' hadn't yet reached these parts. "I'll pay for the call," he said. He raked into a pocket and pulled out a two-pound coin which he placed onto the counter.

"In the back office," she said gesturing to a cramped office space behind her.

"Thanks," he said.

He stepped around the counter, went through an open hatch and into an office space that was crammed with glossy magazines, newspapers, and assorted clutter. She closed the glass door behind him, so at least he had some privacy. The telephone was sitting on the top of a desk. He took DI Welsh's card from a pocket and proceeded to punch the number into the pad. His call was answered on the tenth ring.

"DI Welsh," she announced.

"It's Max Deardon," he said.

"How can I help you?" she asked.

"I think there's something you need to be aware of," he said.

"What is it?"

"I'm with a psychic called Ingrid Prescott. We're in a village called Abbotsford, just a couple of miles from my sister's home. She's convinced there are bodies in a wooded area near by," he said, slightly out of breath.

"Who is?" she asked.

"Ingrid Prescott," he replied.

"Whose bodies?" she asked.

"I don't know. Three people. Two men and a woman. But she doesn't think it's my sister." He felt uneasy saying that. "She's had a psychic premonition. I'd guess you'd call it an event."

"What's the location?" she asked.

"At the back of my sister's home. Down the bottom of the steep hill, about five hundred yards away. What do I need to do now?" he asked.

She didn't respond immediately. She must have been thinking about the question.

"I'll call the local police and ask them to meet you there. I'll try to get there as soon as possible. I'll be about an hour. Where's Ralph Colby?" she asked.

"He's at home. We left him there twenty minutes ago," he said.

"Give me the direction to the field," she asked.

He told her how to find the site, then asked her once again what he should do now. She advised him to return to the place and wait for the local police to arrive. He said all right then ended the conversation.

It took him six minutes to return to the wooded area along the road. He parked in the same patch of dry mud by the iron gate. Beside him, Ingrid hadn't said a word for some time. It was as if she was in some kind of emotional recovery after the premonitions.

With the time only four-fifteen, the sun was still bright, and the shadows were ever so slowly lengthening to cast shadow through the copse. It looked idyllic. It was hard to think that the location may contain dark secrets. A car passed on its way up the hill to Elson. They watched it climb the steep ascent. They waited in silence. Waiting for someone to join them.

It was a further twenty minutes before a car appeared on the crest of the hill and came down the descent. As it reached the bottom of the hill, then they could see it was a police car. The car pulled into the verge on the other side of the road and stopped just a few feet ahead of Max's Audi. It had the markings and livery of the Thames Valley police service on the side.

The uniformed driver got out and ambled across the road. He was a young constable. Not much more than twenty-five years of age. He had all the requisite gear, the stab vest, the silver handcuffs, and the pepper spray lodged in the belt around his waist. He had a communication device walkie-talkie velcroid into position near to his left shoulder.

Max pressed the window button for the two front side windows to slide down. The cop was a handsome young fellow with a dark complexion, dark eyes, dark hair, and a nice smile. He eyed Ingrid first, then looked at the driver.

"I understand you've been in contact with the Met Police," he said. "Something about bodies in a field."

"That's correct," said Max. "This is Ingrid Prescott. She's a psychic."

The cop looked at her for a second time. Ingrid remained silent as if she had no desire or little need to talk to the officer. Max carried on talking. "We believe that there may be bodies in the field. Just over there." He thrust his chin in the direction of the copse.

"Okay," said the constable. He straightened his back to look over the top of the car. He was now stony faced as if he had no idea how he was supposed to react to such a revelation. "Perhaps you can show me the place," he said, then stepped around the front of the car.

"Sure," replied Max. He opened the door and got out of the car just as the young policeman came to him.

Max led him to the gate, through the gap between the post and along the beaten path, through the wooded area, then out into the open space. The officer asked him a number of questions. First, he asked him who he was and what was his connection to Ingrid. Max told him about his missing sister and why he was in the area, following the brief trip to visit his brother-in-law who resided in the big house at the top of the hill.

The cop commented that there was no obvious indication that there were any shallow graves, no sign of recent removed earth or anything like that. Max agreed with him.

The cop walked away from him at a slow pace, took the walkie-talkie and began to speak into the device. Max couldn't hear what he was saying. After a minute he replaced the unit, then he returned to where Max was standing. The air was now becoming chilly and the breeze was picking up so the leaves on the trees were being gently rustled. Max noticed the dampness of the moisture on his shoes.

The constable looked at him. "I've contacted Reading HQ. I've requested that a team of detectives come out to conduct interviews. They should be here in twenty minutes or so. I suggest we wait for them in our cars."

Max nodded his head. Maybe the police officer believed him, or it was just procedure to call out detectives. It was more than likely the latter. The lack of any visible evidence of disturbed earth made the theory less likely to be credible, but the officer didn't know that. Max and the constable walked back along the track and on towards the road.

# Chapter 13

A team of two plain-clothed detectives arrived on the scene around thirty minutes after the young police officer had made the call. They introduced themselves as DI Simon Rogerson and DI Paul Skinner, both of them from the Thames Valley police constabulary.

Rogerson looked to be the older one, perhaps in his early forties. DI Skinner was younger by several years. Both detectives were polished and looked the part. They first consulted with the uniformed officer who gave them the brief details, then they came over to the Audi. In the meantime, the uniformed officer got into his car and left the area.

No sooner had his car disappeared over the crest of the hill, then another car appeared from the direction of Abbotsford and arrived on the scene. It was a silver Vauxhall Astra saloon. It pulled up into the verge in front of Rogerson's and Skinner's grey Volkswagen Passat. The doors opened, and two people got out. One of them was DI Eileen Welsh, the other was a male in civvies. Max was pleased to see Welsh. She knew all about the case, so he wouldn't have to explain it all again to the other detectives. Ingrid and Max had been here for getting on for an hour and they were both becoming tired.

DI Welsh and her companion met with the other plain-clothed local detectives on the other side of the road and had a conversation which was out of earshot of Max and Ingrid. He could only summarise they were discussing Helena's case.

Their conversation didn't last for too long before DI Welsh broke away and stepped across the road to the Audi. She looked ready for action. She was wearing a coffee-coloured trouser suit that fitted a little too tightly around her hips and bust. There was a business-like eagerness on her face. The badge in her jacket lapel glinted.

Max got out of the car. Ingrid remained seated in the front passenger seat. The guy who had arrived with DI Welsh was close to her side. He was young. No more than thirty-two or thirty-three years of age, Max guessed. He was fresh faced, neat, and slender in a light charcoal suit, white shirt and plain tie. With a neat short haircut, he had the appearance of a Jehovah's Witness door knocker.

"This is DI Ray Malik," said DI Welsh. "What have you got?" she asked Max, then glanced into the car at Ingrid.

"That is Ingrid Prescott," he said. "She had a vision that there are several bodies buried in the open area, over there," he broke off to turn his head and nod in the general direction of the wooden area, over his shoulder. The passenger door of the Audi opened, and Ingrid climbed out.

"Hi Ingrid. How are you?" DI Welsh asked her.

"You two know each other?" Max asked in a tone of surprise.

Either, DI Welsh and Ingrid ignored his question or didn't hear him ask it. It must have been the former.

DI's Skinner and Rogerson came across the road and joined the gang of four around the Audi. DI Welsh nor Ingrid Prescott said anything. There was no obvious tension or signs of body language that pointed to a previous acrimonious exchange or anything like that.

"What did you feel?" DI Welsh asked Ingrid.

"A feeling of profound sadness."

"Any visions?" asked Welsh.

"A vison of people digging in this vicinity late in the night or in the early hours of the morning and the vision of a body covered in a blanket," Ingrid said.

"Male or female?" DI Welsh asked.

"The vision was too fleeting," said Ingrid. "But I had a second vision. Men, maybe two or three digging graves in the copse over there."

"Several graves?" DI Malik asked her.

"Yes," she replied.

DI Welsh turned back to Rogerson and Skinner. "Get onto your colleagues. Tell them we have had an indication that there might be one, two, or three bodies in this area," she said. DI Rogerson nodded his head, sagely.

Max was surprised. They were taking Ingrid's premonitions incredibly seriously.

"Anything else?" DI Welsh asked Ingrid.

"The house. The Colby house," she replied.

"What about it?" DI Welsh asked.

"There was a sensation of death in there. I got a feeling that there has been a violent struggle and death in the house in the recent past."

"Death or deaths?" DI Welsh asked.

"Deaths," Ingrid replied.

"More than one?" DI Malik asked seeking confirmation.

"Yes. Maybe as many as two or even three."

Max gulped hard. He could hardly believe it. It didn't seem possible.

"What visions have you had?" DI Welsh asked Ingrid.

"Of a man been held down on his back and several others beating him and kicking him around the head."

"How many men?" DI Malik asked.

"Attackers?" she asked.

"Yes."

"Two or three," she replied.

"Was Ralph Colby with the group of attackers?" DI Welsh asked.

"I didn't see his face," said Ingrid. "Only a grainy image of the men. It was impossible to identify them clearly."

DI Skinner looked to DI Rogerson. "I'd better make that call," he said. "Get some forensic guys down here."

He must have been junior to DI Rogerson for it was DI Skinner who went across the road to their car and climbed inside. Max watched him take a radio receiver and relay a message to police headquarters. They wanted a forensics team on site as soon as possible.

DI Welsh looked into the wooded area. "Ingrid can you take us to the spot where you think the graves are?" she asked.

"They're somewhere in the open area. Over there," she pointed in the direction. "I'll take you."

Ingrid led DIs Welsh, Rogerson, and Malik to the gate, pushed through the narrow gap and onto the track. DI Skinner stayed in his car. Max remained standing by his car. He watched the group go along the track, through the high trees and emerge into the opening. He could see Ingrid spread her hands as if to say somewhere in this area, which must have been forty yards long by twenty yards deep. She had her hands to her temples as if she was trying to revisit the images that had come into her head.

Max noticed the fresh tyre tracks in the earth for the first time. He observed the police officers talking. Ingrid was in the centre of them. He saw her spread her hands for a second time. They were taking her very seriously, so seriously that a forensic team from the Reading headquarters, had been summoned to attend the scene.

To Max, who had not been invited, the discussion seemed to go on for a long time but was only about seven minutes in real time. Then they sauntered back along the track. DI Welsh approached Max and took him aside. She advised him not to divulge any of this to anyone. He agreed. The group broke up within a couple of minutes, and each went their separate ways.

Max drove back into central London with Ingrid by his side. He didn't know where this would end, when or how. He did fear for his sister's wellbeing, but he didn't have the intense fear he had had previously. He now believed Ingrid when she said his sister was alive and safe, or as safe as could be. But he didn't know for certain and that was the thing that gave him cause for concern. Half of him thought she was alive. The other half suspected that she might have been one of the bodies Ingrid Prescott said were buried in the copse.

They were soon in central London. He took Ingrid into Bloomsbury and dropped her off outside the 'Bookworm' book store. From there he made his way the mile or so into Swiss Cottage and home to his flat.

He arrived home at just after six-thirty. Once there, he checked his answer phone for any messages. Rosetta Sanchez had called him and left a message. She wouldn't be returning to London for a while. Her father had been placed on the critical list. She wouldn't be back for at least another six days. He didn't know what to think, say or do. His mind was too consumed with thoughts of the day's events and the question of whether his sister was one of the bodies buried in the wood.

# Chapter 14

Thursday 29th June

On Thursday morning, Max was in the office for seven-forty-five as usual. He got straight down to business and went onto the trading floor to chat to several of the traders. He attempted to be jovial when discussing yesterday and what they had got up to trading wise. A colleague called Jeff Winter asked him what he had done on his day off. Max replied, nothing much. In the back of his mind he couldn't help but wonder where this would end. The only other person who knew about his personal problem was Lloyd Sherwood. Max hoped that he hadn't developed a loose tongue and had began to let out rumours about Max's brother-in-law and sister. But he thought he could trust Lloyd to keep quiet. After all he was his best buddy in the company. Perhaps, he should have a chat to him and put it to him in a friendly manner about the need to keep things around here tight. But he wouldn't.

Ralph Colby hadn't contacted him to ask about Ingrid. That surprised Max to a degree. Ralph liked to come across as the caring, sharing sort of person. Maybe he suspected, or even knew, that Ingrid wasn't his girlfriend, but someone brought in to investigate the disappearance of Helena. He wasn't stupid, but there again why would he think that?

Max wondered whether to contact him to explain why they had left so quickly, blaming it on a sickness bug she had picked up. He decided against it.

During the morning, Jeff Winter came into Max's office for a chat. Winter said that he had heard a rumour that his own application for voluntary redundancy had been approved at the meeting of the senior execs.

The official announcement would be by way of an email, followed by a confirmation letter. Winter said he didn't know if Max's application had been approved or rejected. There was no official word leaking out of the Human Resource team. Sara Lynn, Head of the department, had it watertight up there. Leaks were not flowing out like they did when her predecessor was in post.

By Thursday afternoon Max had not received any word from DI Welsh or anyone else about whether the police were planning to dig up the field to look for the bodies Ingrid said were buried there. Maybe these things took a long time to organise. Or maybe he had been taken out of the loop.

Friday 30th June

Friday soon came around. It was ten o'clock in the morning when he received a call from Sara Lynn to pop into her officer for a brief chat. He said of course he would. This was it he thought. He would learn his fate at a one-to-one.

Jeff Winter and several other colleagues on the same scale as Max had already received their final notification of the decision made by the panel. At the rate at which people were going, there wouldn't be many of his colleagues left by the time the process had been finalised.

Max went to see Sara Lynn. He had a lot of respect for Sara. She was a very pleasant, forty-year-old with a good dress sense. Nice to look at. The kind of lady who looked after herself and took pride in her appearance. She had a couple of children in their teens, though she was now divorced from their father. Max wouldn't mind admitting that he had once fancied her.

She smiled at Max has he entered her office. She was a wannabee artist. Several of her own paintings were dotted around the walls of her office along with her diplomas and whatnot. Glass frame photographs of her children were set on her desk.

The smile soon turned into a more serious face. She got up from behind her desk, carrying a folder in her hand. Rather than sit at her desk, she suggested they go to the round table at which three chairs were placed. She asked him how he was. He said okay.

Before they were seated there was a knock at the door. The door opened, and CEO Petra Devries entered. Max had not expected her but clearly by the three seats around the table, Sara Lynn had.

Petra gave him a toothy grin. He wondered why she had decided to drop in on the one-to-one, which had clearly become a two-on-one. She joined Lynn and Max at the table. In her plush business suit, she was power dressing. He had the impression that he had been ambushed in a pincer movement.

Petra took the file from Sara Lynn, opened it and glanced at the top sheet. She raised her head and began.

"Max. I shan't beat about the bush," she said. "Your application for voluntary redundancy has been rejected by the panel."

Max said nothing. DeVries continued to speak. "The company have a counter offer. We wish to offer you the role of Chief Executive going forward." Petra looked to Sara Lynn. "Perhaps you could explain the reason and the package, Sara."

"Of course," said Sara Lynn. She cleared her throat with a dainty cough. "Petra will be leaving the London office shortly to take up a new role at the cooperate HQ in Zurich. Therefore, the post of Chief Executive Officer of the London office will become vacant. The company wish to offer you the post with effect from the first of August." She paused to wait for a reaction from Max, but he didn't say a word. "The package we wish to offer you is very competitive. You will receive a twenty-five percent increase on your gross salary and other benefits, such as increased annual leave and an improved share option, should you wish to take it up," she added.

He gently nodded his head. In truth he assumed the call from Sara would be to tell him that he was being 'let-go'. The offer of the job as CEO of the London office was a complete turnaround. He was pleasantly surprised but not totally shocked.

"What are the choices?" he asked. The question seemed to come as a surprise to Sara Lynn, but not so much to Petra DeVries.

Lynn quickly recovered her composure. "Of course. You're under no obligation what-so-ever to accept. You can turn it down if you wish," she said.

"Or accept the package," said DeVries. "Perhaps you'd like some time to think about it," she said.

He nodded his head. "What are the timescales for a decision?" he asked.

"Five pm on Monday," said Lynn. "You've got the weekend to think about it," she added.

"What if I turn it down?"

"Your current post is in line for re-assignment," said Sara, which was management speak for it wouldn't be around much longer in the same capacity.

Petra DeVries sat forward and placed her thick forearms onto the glass top. "The company is restructuring its operation here in London as a consequence of the Brexit vote we're downsizing, but still intend to maintain a presence in London," she said.

"I should hope so," said Max. "With all due respect, Brexit or no Brexit, London will still be a big player in our business," he said.

"I couldn't agree more," said Petra DeVries. "But in anticipation of some of our customers going to Frankfurt, we're realigning our strategy. We still see London as a major centre."

Deardon didn't think she knew what she was talking about but remained tight lipped. "What if I decide to reject your offer?" he asked.

Petra DeVries coughed. "First of all, we'll be very disappointed to lose you," she said. "We value your expertise, dedication, and work ethic." *Leave it out*, he thought. "If you turn down the post, you'll be let-go and be entitled to redundancy, but you won't be given the enhanced package."

"Have a think about it," said Sara Lynn in a soothing tone of voice.

"I certainly will," he said. In reality it was a 'no-brainer'. He had to accept the offer, but something in the back of his mind left a nagging doubt. He assumed that Petra DeVries and Sara Lynn would see his reticence to accept the offer immediately as a delaying tactic aimed at getting an increase from twenty-five percent to say nearer to thirty-five, but it was nothing of the sort.

"Do you have any questions?" Sara Lynn asked.

"Who are remaining at my level?" he asked.

Lynn glanced at Petra DeVries.

"We're letting half of the level go," said DeVries. "Then we shall be promoting new talent from within the firm. The overall team in the London office will be trimmed by twenty percent, but we anticipate a downturn of around fifteen percent in activity due to some investors moving out of the London market."

"I'm not sure it will be that high," he said.

"That's why we require you to stay," said DeVries, with genuine praise in her tone. "But of course. It's completely up to you. It's your decision," she said.

She closed the file and shifted it across the desk to Sara Lynn. It was almost as if she was saying. It's now over to you to convince him, but that wasn't Sara's style. DeVries stood up, followed by Sara Lynn. Max got to his feet. He thanked them for keeping him informed and up to date. If they were expecting him to give them a decision here and now they were going to be disappointed, but he doubted that that was the case. They knew he was a careful man.

"I'll let you know by five o'clock on Monday evening," he said. It was an opportunity of a lifetime and one to further his career, but he wasn't sure if he wanted to take it on when a lot of the people he knew would be moving on. He left Sara Lynn's office and went down one floor to the trading floor and stepped into his office.

# Chapter 15

Once back at his desk he slumped into his deep, black-leather armchair and looked at his PC screen. The numbers on the screen were mostly in a shade of white-yellow. Then he looked out of the window on the twentieth floor of the building and across the spread of the city as it converged into one giant urban landscape of high rise tower blocks, church steeples, and industrial facilities.

He wanted to call DI Welsh but decided against it. Today was three weeks since he had received the telephone call from Ralph Colby to tell him that his sister had left him. The knot in his stomach was the sensation of fear that, despite what Ingrid Prescott said, his sister would be found in a shallow grave in the field at the bottom of the long rolling hillside just five hundred yards from her home.

After chewing over it for a while he made the call at eleven o'clock to DI Welsh. She didn't pick it up, so he couldn't do anything else but leave a message on her voice mail. He asked her to call him when she was free. He thanked her then hung up.

It was with some surprise when, forty-five minutes later, DI Welsh returned his call. She told him of the progress or, rather the lack of it. A finger-tip examination of the parcel of field that Ingrid said contained one or more shallow graves, had been examined by members of the Thames Valley police forensic team. Several items of interest had been found that indicated the possibility of some activity, but that's all it was, just a possibility. The items were currently under examination. The outcome of the tests would determine if the field was to be excavated. She promised to call him should there be a development. He somehow doubted that that would happen.

At twelve noon there was a knock at the door to his office.

"Come in," he said out loud. The door open. Lloyd Sherwood put his head around the frame. Max invited him to take a seat by his desk. Lloyd was looking unusually stressed and haggard. His usual smile was a trifle strained.

"What can I do for you?" Max asked.

"They've turned me down for voluntary redundancy," Lloyd said.

"You too?"

"You as well?" said Lloyd, running a hand over the back of his neck.

"Me as well," said Max. "I've been granted a stay of execution until Monday evening at least." He didn't want to tell him that he had been offered the CEO's job, until he had either turned it down or accepted the offer.

Lloyd adjusted his position in the seat. "This isn't the real reason why I've come to visit you," he said.

"Shoot," encouraged Max.

"Steve Chilton's been in touch. He's got some information he wants to pass on to you face-to-face, so to speak."

"When?" Max asked.

"In an hour or two."

"Where?" Max asked.

"The same place. The bench on the path by the river."

"Okay. What's it about?"

"He didn't say," said Lloyd. "It must be important though."

"That's true," said Max. He was intrigued. He thanked Lloyd. Lloyd said he would contact Chilton to confirm they would be there.

The remainder of the morning was just like another Friday. There was sporadic trading on the floor. The big news on the financial scene was coming from the Far East. The Nikkei had closed down on the day's trading on news of a fall in Japanese manufacturing output. The number of jobs growth in the US had declined for the third month in a row. This may influence the British market, though the change could be minimal. The British economy was still doing well. The FTSE had closed up yesterday, by point six of one percent on trading the day before.

Lloyd returned to collect Max at quarter to one. They left the office five minutes later and walked onto the streets of the City along Cheapside, down a street onto Queen Victoria Street and onto the path that led to the bridge. A cool breeze had people eagerly reaching for warm fleeces and jumpers. For a day in late June, it wasn't packed with tourists. There appeared to be just as many street entertainers as on-lookers.

They cut down the walkway towards the river, down the steps and onto the path, then along the side of the river and towards the bench they had sat on before.

The private detective, Steve Chilton was already sitting on the bench. It was the first time Max had seen him since this time last week. He was dressed in jeans and a shiny grey puffer jacket. He had designer, dark shades over his eyes. The breeze was blowing through his hair. He had a document holder by his side.

Max and Sherwood approached him and sat down one at each side of him. A boat on the river sounded its horn. The gulls perched on the silver metal cables on the bridge flew off, startled by the sound.

"How are you?" Chilton asked Max.

"Okay," he replied. "I understand that you've got some fresh information."

"Just thought I'd keep you up to speed," said Chilton. "I've got something I heard about your brother-in-law."

"What is it?" Max asked.

"Juicy."

"How juicy?"

"We know from a contact that Colby's been a regular guest at parties given by Louis Delaney."

"What kind of parties?" Max asked.

"Delaney organises orgies and sex parties. He ships in girls for his friends and other invited guests. Apparently, it's something like that movie, 'Eyes Wide Shut'. Have you seen it?" he asked.

"Yeah. I think so. From what I recall it's about a guy who bluffs his way into a party and all the guests are watching couples having sex or something like that," said Max.

"It's got Tom Cruise and Nicole, what's-her-face, in it. These parties are like that. A load of rich blokes getting their rocks off with these birds. Delaney facilitates them. He's got the great and the good at these dos. The birds are usually bare-arse naked or close to. All the guys wear these fancy Venetian masks and cloaks. The name of the game is to get drunk or high then take a girl to a room and screw her. Or they all end up in a room screwing each other."

"Oh my God," said Max. "And Ralph Colby attends these...*parties*?" he said parties after a pause to try and think of another word but couldn't think of one.

"That's what Louis Delaney puts on. Something very similar," said Chilton. He calls them the, 'Other Side of Midnight' parties."

"It sounds as if Colby and this Louis Delaney know each other well," Max said.

"That would appear to the case," said Chilton. He took his shades off, licked the lenses, then wiped them on a piece of soft cloth in his pocket. He continued. "I reckon the police have found something in the field, but they're not telling anyone until they have a positive identification," he said.

"How do you know about that?" Max asked. He wondered if Lloyd Sherwood had told him, but then he realised he hadn't told Lloyd a thing, so Chilton couldn't have got it from him. It must have been Ingrid Prescott.

"I've heard nothing for certain," Chilton said.

"DI Welsh told me she'd let me know, but I think she's just saying that to keep me quiet," Max said.

"They'll tell you jack shit. That's the way they work," Chilton said, as if he knew how these things work. "Ingrid has been very accurate in the past with her premonitions. She's an amazing lady," he added.

"You're not kidding," said Max. "Her powers are incredible."

"She's got a reputation of being right on these things," said Chilton. He had finished wiping his shades and replaced them over his eyes.

"DI Welsh seems to know her," said Max. "I was quite surprised by that. She must be aware of her ability to see visions."

"Some police forces are using psychic's increasingly on cold cases," said Chilton.

"I didn't know that," said Max.

"You won't. Unless you're involved in police work," said Chilton. He got up from off the bench and rubbed his back. He took a step to the edge of the path, put both hands on the top of the barrier and looked down onto the choppy brown waves of the river. He turned back to the bench and glanced at his watch.

"Sorry. I have to go. I'll keep you informed if I hear anything else about your brother-in-law," he said.

"Thanks," said Max, slightly surprised by his haste to leave.

Chilton bade both Max and Lloyd farewell, then he took off to walk along the path towards the steps leading up to the start of the Millennium Bridge walkway.

Max and Lloyd watched him go up the steps and disappear out of view. Max could hardly believe that Ralph Colby would take part in such sordid activities as sex parties and orgies, but maybe he shouldn't be surprised at anything anymore. He wondered if Helena had learned off these activities and had left him, or if she had confronted her husband. Maybe, instead of repenting and telling her he would stop attending, he had told her he wouldn't or maybe worse. Maybe he had killed her for she would have had good grounds for a separation and divorce. Max chastised himself. His imagination was beginning to run away from him.

Lloyd and Max walked back to the office. The meeting with Chilton had not lasted long, but he had learned some more revealing information about his brother-in-law.

# Chapter 16

The volume of trading on Friday morning had been busy, but by the afternoon it had become less active. It was nothing unusual. Friday afternoons tended to wind down from around two o'clock onwards, though some could be frenetic. This wasn't one of them.

Max had a couple of emails in his in-box, but nothing that required his immediate attention. He was daydreaming somewhat, standing at the window, looking out onto the river and the stretch up to Tower Bridge in the near distance. He had enjoyed this view for the past three years. If he took the CEO job, he would be one floor up. But something in the back of his mind was telling him it was time to move on. He wasn't getting any younger. It was becoming a young man's game. He didn't know if he had the energy or the desire to do the job. In this moment, he made up his mind to turn the job down. He would inform Petra DeVries and Sara Lynn that he wouldn't be taking up their kind offer.

His telephone rang. He returned to his desk, sat in the leather swivel chair, reached out and tapped the loudspeaker button. The number in the panel looked familiar, but he couldn't place it straight off.

"Max Deardon," he said looking at the plastic mesh over the number panel. "How can I assist you?" he asked.

"Max. Is that you?" enquired a distant voice. The tone of voice sounded familiar, but it was too short to put a face to it.

"Who is it?" he asked.

"Why, it's Helena," said the voice in a tone that was surprised that he hadn't recognised it.

Max was confused. It took a moment for the penny to drop. "Helena. Oh my God. You're safe? Where are you?" he asked. "Where have you been?" The questions fell out of his mouth in a cascade of combined joy and shock.

"I've been away for a while," she replied. She sounded distance. Like she was on the other side of the world.

"I know. I've been worried sick. I can't believe it's you," he said.

"It's definitely me," she said. "Why have you been worried sick?" she asked.

"Because I had no idea where you were. You don't know what I've been through. I've been to hell and back," he said.

"Don't be worried. I'm fine," she reassured him.

The reality of who he was talking to hit him square on the jaw. "Oh my God!" He took in a deep breath.

"Sorry," she said.

Then the anger came tumbling out. "Sorry. Is that all you can say? I've been imagining all sorts of things," he said in an emotional outburst.

"I had to leave Ralph and go away for a while," she said.

"Why?" he asked.

"I needed a break."

"Have you called him yet?" Max asked.

"No. Not yet. I've tried to contact him at home, at his practice and in the Barbican flat, but he's not at any of them."

"What about his smart phone?"

"It's turned off," she said.

"What's been the problem?" he asked.

"My marriage to him has been a little strained recently. I wanted to get away to create some distance, so I didn't tell him where I'd gone," she said.

"Where have you been staying?" he asked.

"I rented a cottage on the Yorkshire Moors. Near to where our parents took us."

"The Yorkshire Moors?"

"Yes. The Moors. Whitby is about ten miles away. I've been here thinking about my life and things."

"What things?"

"The work-life balance. Relationships. The future. All that kind of thing," she said.

He suddenly recalled DI Welsh telling him that Ralph had told her Helena had left him for another man.

"Tell me. Are you on your own?" he asked, hardly able to ask the question in case she reacted angrily.

"Of course," she said. "Why do you ask?"

"No reason," he replied. Either she was lying, which he doubted, or Ralph had made it up to get the police off his back. It was probably the latter.

"Why didn't you contact me?" he asked.

"I didn't want to upset you," she said.

"When are you coming home?"

"Tonight. I'm getting the eight-thirty train from York."

Max sucked in a deep breath. "Thank God your safe."

"I'm one hundred and ten percent fine," she said.

"Thank God." She said nothing. "Do you want me to tell Ralph?" he asked.

"You can do if you want," she replied. "You know. He's possibly got himself into some kind of trouble," she said.

"No. What kind of trouble?" he asked.

"I don't know for sure. He seems to have changed in the past six months. He's no longer carefree. Something has gotten to him," she said.

"Is he in danger?"

"More like trouble."

"Who with?" he asked.

"Maybe one of his clients. I don't know. He's clammed up. Wouldn't discuss it with me," she said.

"Has he been seeing anyone else?" Max asked.

"Another woman?" she asked incredulously.

"Yes."

"I don't think so," she said. "Why do you ask?"

He didn't know what to think or what to say. "No reason," he said as if it was an afterthought.

"Look," she said. "I'm heading back to London in the next few hours. I'm shortly on my way to Whitby railway station to catch a train to Middlesbrough, then to York. When I'm home, I'll call you," she said.

"What time do you get into London?" he asked.

"Later on tonight, at around eleven. I think," she said, as if she was not certain.

"Keep your phone on," he said.

"I've had my phone off the past four weeks. I now know I don't need one…"

"I know. I've been trying to contact you. Please keep it on in case I need to contact you urgently. The truth is I've been to the police to report you as missing. Your name is on the Met's missing person list," he revealed.

She didn't respond to this disclosure.

"I'll ring off," she said. "I'll call you later tonight when I'm home." The line went dead.

He wanted to ask her a thousand questions, but she was gone. She didn't sound as if she was under any duress. She wasn't being told what to say by someone standing over her. Her tone of voice was normal. She was in charge. If she had been under any duress, he would have heard it in her voice.

He wondered what to do. He had several options. His priority was to call DI Welsh to inform her that he had heard from Helena, and that she was alive and well, then he would contact Ralph to tell him.

His instinct was to call Ralph first. He put a call into his studio, but there was no response, then he remembered it was Friday. The studio was closed on Friday. He then rang the number of the house in Berkshire, but he got no reply there. He ended the call before the voice mail kicked in. Next, he found DI Welsh's business card and tapped her smart phone number into the number pad. That went straight to voicemail. He composed himself and said.

"Hi. It's Max Deardon. I've got some great news. I've just had a telephone conversation with Helena. She's okay. That's all. You can take her details off the missing person list."

He ended the call. There was so much going on in his head right now. He had to get out and go home. He called Toby to tell him he wasn't feeling well and would be heading home early this evening. The time was getting on for four-thirty.

# Chapter 17

From the City, Max took a cab home to Swiss Cottage. On arriving home, he made himself something to eat, then tidied his flat, though it wasn't untidy. He did a few small tasks he had been meaning to do for a while, then he washed some dishes and generally did several house-cleaning tasks.

It was getting on for six o'clock when he put in a call to Ralph. Ralph picked up the telephone on the third ring.

"Ralph?"

"Yes."

"It's Max. I've got some news."

"What?" asked Colby.

"Helena's called me."

Ralph took in a deep breath. "Is she okay?"

"Yes."

"Where is she?" he asked.

"She's on her way home. What are you doing now?" Max enquired.

"Nothing much. Watching TV," said Colby.

"Why don't I drive over to your place? It's easier chatting to you one-to-one rather than over the telephone."

Colby thought about it for a few moments. "Okay. Fine. Come over."

"I'll be there in an hour," said Max.

"Will you be on your own this time?"

"Yes."

"No new girlfriend?" Colby asked.

"No."

"Okay."

"I'll see you in an hour," said Max. He ended the call.

He left his flat ten minutes later, taking his car keys and the key to his garage which was at the rear of the building.

The traffic, for a Friday evening, wasn't too bad. He made his way through the dregs of the evening rush hour towards the west side of the city and out onto the M4. He checked his phone for any missed calls. He didn't have any.

After passing the turn-offs for Heathrow airport, the traffic heading west thinned out. He increased his pace and was close to the first turn off into the Reading area. Rather than take the second turn off into the town, he elected to take the first exit and head towards the village of Abbottsford. This way he would be able to drive passed the field and see if there was any police activity.

He soon made it to Abbotsford. He passed the village pub and reached the junction with the left turn onto the road leading into the village of Elson. On the corner was the old petrol station, now the antiques store. It was about three hundred yards further down the road, where a row of houses ended, that he saw the sign in the verge. It read: *'Road ahead closed - Diversion in place.'*

He continued for another mile. In the distance was the rolling hillside giving a vista onto a valley plain that stretched for miles into the distance.

He drove onward, passing another sign then he came to the barrier across the road. It simply said, *'Thames Valley Police - Road Closed - no way through.'*

The wooded area was only another five or six hundred yards ahead. He could just make out a line of vehicles in the distance, parked along the road. And what looked like erected floodlights in the field. But it was too far to make them out clearly. He stopped in front of the barrier and took his smart phone. The strength of the signal was so poor there was no way he could make a call.

He couldn't do anything but do a three-point turn and go back into Abbotsford. He took the right turn into the village. There was another narrow road, nothing much better than a farmer's track that would take him into Elson, so he had little option but to take it.

All the time he was thinking about the conversation with Helena and what she said about Ralph being in some kind of trouble. He didn't know if he would raise the matter with him. Attending sex parties with the likes of well-known criminals was his own private business. He wouldn't raise it unless Ralph mentioned it first.

It took him around ten minutes to circumnavigate the tight country lanes. The time was getting on for ten past seven. The sunlight was drifting in the cloudy sky and dropping lower so there was a haze of soft yellow light spread over the fields. It was a very delightful picturesque evening.

He ascended the steep hillside, took a right turn onto the road that led into Elson and headed into the hamlet of fifteen houses. He drove through the village with its thatched roof cottages and old worldly charm and character. In the next minute he passed the road descending down to the wooded enclosure. There was a sign at the top saying: '*Thames Valley Police - Road Closed – no through way*'.

The police must have been searching the copse looking for the bodies Ingrid Prescott said were buried there.

He came to the sharp right-left dog-leg in the road and came to the front of the Colby house. He drove straight through the open gate and onto the forecourt. It had been about an hour since he had spoken to Colby on the telephone.

# Chapter 18

Colby's BMW was parked by the entrance under the porch. Max pulled up next to it and killed the engine. He composed himself, wondering how he would raise the topic of why Helena had left the home.

A moment passed then the front door opened. Colby appeared under the shade of the porch. He was dressed casually in a loose-fitting shirt and stripy, knee length shorts. He was holding a glass generously filled with what could have been brandy. He looked chilled and carefree.

Max got out of his car and advanced to the front door. There was no expression on Colby's face.

"You on your own?" Colby asked. "No lady with you this time?"

"I'm on my jack jones."

Colby led him through the hallway and into the wide reception area. On the left was the closed door into the kitchen, then the stairs which turned at a landing on their way to the first floor. The doors into the other rooms were closed except for the sitting room. Light was streaming in through the doorway at the back of the house. Colby went into the sitting room. Max followed him inside. He headed for the sofa and sat down, whilst Colby backed to the French windows, but remained standing. Glossy magazines, some trade papers and personal papers were scattered over the surface of the glass topped coffee table in front of the sofa.

"What can I do for you?" asked Colby in a relaxed and open tone of voice. He took a sip of the liquid in the glass. By the rosy glow to his cheeks, it didn't look as if it was his first drink of the day.

"Helena called me," said Max. Colby didn't bat an eyelid or reply which Max thought was odd. Maybe the alcohol in his blood had deadened his sense of emotion. "She told me that you're in some kind of trouble," he said. He had planned to skirt around the issue, but his peevishness to know what was going on had got the better of him, so he had got straight down to what was on his mind.

"Ah," said Colby. He stepped back a few paces and dropped into an armchair that was in front of the French windows. The horizontal blinds were open so the glint of the sunlight reflecting on the surface of the pool was visible.

"Trouble might be a bit over dramatic," he said. "What did she tell you?" he enquired. His body language didn't reveal any great tension or anxiety. The alcohol must have been acting as a kind of barrier, though he looked thoughtful as if he was considering his options.

"I'm not prying into your business, but if you're in some kind of trouble maybe I can help you," said Max.

Colby put the rim of the glass to his lips and took a sip of the liquid. His hand appeared to be trembling. Max was longing to ask him about the supposed connection to some London villains, but he elected to hold back. He wanted Colby to tell him.

Colby put the near empty glass onto a side table. He crossed his legs. His bony left knee was prominent. The light was reflecting on his balding pate. He was saying nothing.

"This trouble you're in does it have something to do with some East End villains?" Max had asked the question.

Colby smiled. "I wouldn't call them that. I would refer to them as charming business associates," he said.

Max decided to reveal his hand. "Two guys called Louis Delaney and Eric Lomax."

Colby tensed a little. He dropped the pretence. His expression became serious and questioning. "Where did you get those names?" he asked.

"I've heard the names from a couple of people. Do you care to tell me how you know them?" Max asked.

Colby reached for the glass, took it in his hand, lifted it to his lips, but put it down on the table top. He sat back, uncrossed his legs, and stretched them out. His brother-in-law waited for an answer.

"I've treated Delaney's daughter," he said. "That's how I met him. He's been in the studio a few times. I know him as a man of enterprise. I found him to be a nice guy. We talked for a while in my office. Became friends. After all he is paying for his daughter's treatment. It isn't cheap. She is having her jaw realigned to make her looks far smoother. It's all to aid her sales potential…"

"And?" Max asked butting in.

"And, he invited me to attend a party at his house." He paused to run a hand across his mouth. His voice had become a little strained and tense. The alcohol was slurring his words but not enough that he couldn't be understood.

"Are these parties called the *other side of midnight*, or something like that?" Max asked.

"Yeah. How do you know?" Colby asked.

Max thought about his response. "Let's just say it's something I picked up. What are these parties like?"

"All the participants must have a mask and a cape. It's a bit like a Caligari theme party. I'd think you'd say."

Max tried to make a connection and picture the scene in his mind's eye. "Who supplies the girls?"

"Delaney does. All the girls are how can I say…Girls of easy virtue and loose morals."

"Sex parties?" Max asked.

Colby smiled. "Well, they're not cultural exchanges."

"What happens?"

"What happens?" Colby asked in a rhetorical tone. "What doesn't? Use your imagination."

He took the glass from the side table, put the rim to his lips and drained the remaining contents. His face looked reflective.

"Did something happen at the party?"

Colby gave him a quarter smile. "I was introduced to this delightful creature. She called herself a model."

"Is that it?" Max asked.

"We had sex a couple of times."

"Do you love her?"

"Don't be so melodramatic," he scolded.

"What timescale are we talking about here?"

"It was about this time last year," Colby replied.

"Did Helena suspect you?"

"No. Of course not. Helena was away on one of her trips."

"So, you met a girl at one of the parties, and you had consensual sex with her. Did it end there?"

"I wish it had," Colby said in a pinched tone. "I saw her a few times in town. We even went out to dinner on a couple of occasions."

Max noticed the past tense. He was put on edge.

"And Helena didn't suspect a thing?" Max asked again.

"I was careful. Anyway, I don't think she would have cared. Our marriage hasn't been a marriage in the conventional sense of the word for some time," he admitted.

"This girl. Do you still see her?" Max asked.

"No."

"Why is that?"

Colby sat forward. "Can I get you a drink?" he asked. "I'm having a refill. A whisky, a brandy, a coffee, a juice or any kind."

Max's throat was dry. "A glass of orange would be nice," he said.

"Just bear with me one minute," said Colby. He got up from his seat, taking his empty glass with him. Max watched him go out of the door and step out of the room. He could hear the patter of his feet in the reception room, then the door to the kitchen open.

Max got up off the sofa and advanced across the room to the French windows that opened onto a patio area in front of the swimming pool. A rattan lounger was on the patio. A springboard stretched over the pool edge. Across on the other side was the wide garden, about fifty yards long, to the screen of tall trees at the boundary of the property. The trees were a shield that provided an element of security before the hillside as it began to slide down to the wood at the bottom of the hill.

If the rectangle of open area was being excavated, then maybe Colby had noticed the activity. Or maybe he hadn't. There was no indication in his manner that he had. Max turned back. He sat down on the sofa as Colby came back into the room. He was carrying a fresh glass of brandy in one hand and a slim glass of orange juice in the other.

He came to Max and handed him the glass. Then he went back to his seat and sat down.

"These parties. How many did you attend?" Max asked.

"Two or three," he replied.

"This girl. Do you still see her?"

"Not anymore."

"Why? Did you call it off?"

"You could say that."

Max put the glass to his lips and took a sip of the drink. The fresh orange tasted nice. The tangy flavour burst on the back of his tongue.

"Were there any more girls you met?" he asked.

"No," replied Colby. He had the rim of the refill at his lips, but he hadn't taken a sip of the liquor.

"If you didn't call it off and Helena didn't find out. How come you don't see her anymore?"

"How's your drink?" Colby asked.

"Fine."

"Long story," said Colby, replying to the question.

"Care to share it?"

"Do I care to share it?" He asked rhetorically. "Maybe I do. Maybe I don't."

He took a long intake of the brandy, taking in half of the contents in one long gulp.

Max did likewise with the juice. The orange bits became trapped in his teeth.

"So where is the girl?" he asked.

"She's dead," Colby replied.

"What?" Max spluttered. "How?"

Colby crossed his legs. "Before I tell you. I really ought to ask you not to breath a word of this to anyone. Promise?" he asked.

The chime of the carriage clock on the mantel piece, below the long mirror chimed on the half hour. It was seven-thirty.

Max suddenly felt a tightening in his chest. Over the next ten seconds the pressing sensation intensified. He put the rim of the glass to his mouth and took in a good proportion of the liquid. A tangy almond taste hit the back of his tongue.

Colby watched him closely. "The girl is dead because someone killed her," he said.

"Who?" asked Max.

Colby didn't reply directly to the question. "Before I tell you, let's finish our drinks," he said.

He lifted the glass to his mouth and took in a mouthful. Max did likewise. There was about one third of the liquid remaining in the glass. He had drunk two thirds. Maybe more.

Colby climbed out of the chair. He turned to face the French windows and looked out onto the patio by the swimming pool. His back was to Max, so his outline was silhouetted against the bright light. Then he turned back to face him.

"It should be working by now," he said.

"What?" asked Max. He was still aware of the pressure in his chest and an increasing sense and feeling of nausea in his nostrils and mouth. He had a word at the end of his tongue, but he couldn't force it out of his mouth. His eyelids suddenly felt heavy. There was a mist before his eyes and in his head. He looked at Colby whose form suddenly became double. Colby's body zoomed in and out of focus and from side to side.

"W...W...W...K...K...K" he said in a garbled word of nonsense. Colby's distant form moved closer and closer to him until he was standing over him and looking down into his face.

"Who killed the girl?" Colby repeated the question back to Max. His words seemed to be at a distance then came bouncing back as if he was in an echo chamber.

Max's head dropped to a side and he went as limp as a rag doll.

# Chapter 19

When Max regained consciousness, he found himself in a cold, dark, and damp place. He felt queasy. The throb at his temples was like nothing he had felt before. A mist swirled in front of his eyes. He felt as if he had the worst hangover he had ever experienced in his life. He tried to move his arms, but his wrists were secured to the armrest of the seat he was propped up in. His legs were stretched out. He felt cold and shivered. His body was covered in a coat of sweat. He had been stripped of the top half of his clothing. He attempted to move his hands for a second time, but they were secured to the seat by straps around his wrists. Then he was aware of the strap around his forehead which was securing his head to a headrest. The air smelled fusty. He was in a cellar or a basement or even a dungeon. He had no idea how long he had been out.

An overhead light suddenly came on. Followed by the sound of a door opening on his left side, then the sound of feet on a solid surface. He could see that he was strapped to a dentist's chair. From what he could tell the room had plain white plasterboard walls. Because of the strap holding his head in place, he couldn't look up or down or from side to side. He could see that the toes of his shoes were scuffed, as if he had been dragged. Then, and only then, was he aware of the device in his mouth which was keeping his mouth wide open. He couldn't close his jaws.

Then a figure in white came to hover over him and look into his face.

"How are you doing?" Ralph Colby asked. He was dressed in a white dentist's smock. He had a mask over his mouth, a round cap on his head and thick wide lens surgeon's glasses over his eyes.

Max attempted to move his hands for a third time, but he couldn't get any purchase under the straps, though he was aware that the strap on the left-hand side was loose under the armrest.

"There's no need to struggle," said Colby. "She was blackmailing me," he said. "It happened right here in this house. I didn't want it to happen, but I had to stop her. I put my hands around her neck. I strangled her to death," he said.

His words were dull against the walls which must have been solid brick behind the plasterboard. Max tried to nod his head but couldn't move it. The device in his mouth was starting to make his jaws ache. Every cell in his body seemed to be crying out for an end to his torture.

Colby put a tool into his mouth. "I killed her. I panicked. I called Louis Delaney for help. He came with two men. They helped me. We buried her in the wood at the bottom of the hill," he said.

Max tried once again to turn his head but couldn't. He struggled in the seat. He pulled on the restraint. The left-hand side felt as if the material holding it in place was becoming less secure.

Colby backed off and stood straight. He moved a tray, that held a multitude of dental implements on it and swung it round so it was close to Max's left side.

161

"The problem was that Delaney had me over a barrel. Not only did he insist that his daughter's fees were zero, he talked me into performing surgery on two people. I had to build this place in the cellar. I had to extract all the teeth of two men without anaesthetic. Their pain was horrendous. Delaney and two of his people were watching. The men were begging for death, so Delaney took them outside into the garden and shot them both. They are also buried in that wooded area. That's where I'll have to bury you," he said.

He took a syringe off the tray and put the tip of the needle into Max's left arm. Max felt the needle puncture his skin. Colby entered the contents in the syringe into his blood stream.

Colby moved away from him. In the next moment the light went out and the door was closed. Max frantically tugged at the straps holding his wrists tight. He could feel it coming loose, but then he felt groggy. His thoughts and movements became laboured. Within a matter of twenty seconds, he passed out and drifted off into a swirl of unconnected thoughts and images in his head. He lost consciousness for a second time.

Max opened his eyes, but instantly closed them because of the bright white light blinding him. He could make out the shape of Colby in his white dentist smock, bearing down on him. He was still strapped to the chair. Colby had put a tool in his mouth that he was using to tap his back teeth. He seemed as if he was about to perform a dental procedure. The plastic device in his mouth to keep his jaws open was still in place. He couldn't talk. All he could do was gargle. He attempted to move his head.

"Stay still," Colby instructed. He jabbed the sharp end of a tool into his gum. Max's mouth exploded with pain. He instantly raised his body and jolted his arms upward with the shock. Such was the force of his movement that the webbing holding the strap to the underside of the chair at his left wrist snapped and came free.

The tray holding several tools was to Max's left side. He instinctively reached out with his left hand and grabbed one of the implements. He could feel its cold metal stem. Taking it in the ball of his hand he swung the point around and buried the end into Colby's arm.

Colby was powerless to stop it. Max felt the tip of the tool go directly into his bicep and deep into the flesh at a point about halfway between his elbow and shoulder.

Colby let out a piercing scream. He instantly staggered back. The tray holding the implements was tipped over. All the items fell onto the floor with a tinny clatter. Colby thrust his left hand to his right arm and attempted to prise the implement out of his flesh. It had gone into his bicep with such force that only half of the stem was visible. As he staggered back, his legs buckled, and he dropped to his knees. He let out another scream that reverberated around the room.

Max was able to use his free hand to take the strap around his forehead and prise it off. In front of him, Colby was attempting to get to his feet. He still had his left hand clamped around the tool protruding out of his arm. Blood was streaming out of the wound. The tool was in so deep he couldn't get enough purchase on it to pull it out.

Meanwhile, Max was able to use his free hand to undo the buckle holding his right hand to the armrest. When his hands were free he sprung out of the chair, took the plastic device holding his mouth ajar and pulled it out.

Colby was now on his haunches. His head was down. As he jumped out of the chair Max swung his left foot and kicked Colby around the head. Colby was sent spinning to the cold, concrete floor.

Max saw his chance to escape. Despite feeling dizzy, he stepped through the open door and out onto a corridor. To the left was a wooden, five-step ascent to an open door. He went along the corridor to the steps, took them two at a time, stepped through the open door and found himself in a dark room. It took him a few moments to realise he was in the kitchen. Directly ahead was a window. The blind was up. The dark of evening was visible beyond the glass.

Turning back, he saw Colby emerge out of the dungeon and advance towards the steps. He had his head down. His left hand was clasped around his bicep where the scalpel had gone into his flesh. He must have been in excruciating pain. Blood was seeping out through the gaps between his fingers. He was breathing in short sharp bursts and wincing. He raised his head and looked at Max standing over the open doorway. He paused. Max felt the urge to jump down and aim several blows at his head, but he elected to stay put and kick him in the chest as soon as he attempted to climb the stairs. Then he looked at the open door and saw the key in the lock. He took the flimsy door and slammed it closed. He felt for the key in the keyhole, gave it a turn and locked the door.

He looked around the kitchen. In the dark and in his confused state, he couldn't make out the fixtures and fittings. The ache in his mouth were Colby had jabbed him with the sharp tool was only now starting to fade. He moved a few paces to the window where there was a sink, double drainer and tap. He ran the tap, scooped up a handful of water in his hand and threw it over his face. Then turning away, he stepped towards the open door that led into the central reception area, felt for the light switch, and turned it on. The lights flickered into action and illuminated the kitchen. He could hear his heart beat pounding in his chest. He could hear whimpering coming from behind the door to the cellar. The door handle went down, but the door remained closed. Colby banged on the flimsy panel and gave it a clout. He shrieked out like a mad man.

# Chapter 20

Max knew he had to get help before Colby worked out a way of being able to get out of the cellar. He went out of the kitchen, across the reception area and into the sitting room. The room was in darkness. He quickly found the light switch and turned it on. Two lampstands, one at each end of the sofa, came on to illuminate the room. He looked around. He couldn't recall where the landline telephone was. His mind was disoriented and confused. Then came the sound of a thud coming from the kitchen. Colby may have been using something he found in the room to ram it against the frame. It took Max a few moments to find a telephone. It was one of those modern mobile units placed in a charger. He went to the sideboard, took the unit, and pressed 9-9-9 into the number pad.

The operator was soon on the line enquiring which service he required.

"Police," he said breathlessly.

"One moment please," said the operator.

A few moments passed, then a new voice came over the line. "How can I help you?" a female operator asked.

"Someone has attempted to murder me," Max said.

"What's your name?" she asked.

"Max Deardon."

"What number are you calling from?" she asked.

"I don't know. It's my sister's home. I've forgotten the number."

"What's the address?"

"It's in Elson. It's the Colby residence. Five to six miles outside of Reading. I'd think," he said.

"You say someone has attempted to murder you?" she asked, as if she didn't believe him.

"Yes."

"Who?"

"My brother-in-law."

"What's his name?" she asked.

"Ralph Colby-Lewis," he replied. "Please hurry. I've managed to lock him in a cellar. He's trying to get out. I've stabbed him in the arm."

"You've locked him in a cellar and stabbed him in the arm?" she asked.

"Yes."

"What with?" she asked.

"A scalpel. A dental tool. I don't know," he snapped.

"What's the address?" she asked again.

"The Colby residence. It's got a Tudor front. As you go through Elson its straight on. After the turn to err…" He couldn't recall the name of the next village. His mind was racing away from him. "Please be quick," he pleaded.

"We'll get someone there as quickly as possible. You say you stabbed him? Is that right?" she asked.

"Yeah."

"Where?" she asked.

"In the cellar under the house," he replied.

"No. Where in his body?" she asked.

"In his arm. He drugged me. Then strapped me to a chair. Is someone coming?" he asked.

"I've despatched a unit to get to you as soon as possible."

"He's admitted to me that he murdered a girl. Right here in the house," Max said.

"Which girl?"

"I don't know. He never told me her name. Someone he met at a party," he said.

"He's told you he's murdered someone?" she asked.

"Yes. Plus, he knows of two other people who've been buried in a shallow grave in a wooded copse at the bottom of the hill," he said.

The thud-thud-thud coming from the kitchen was continuing. It sounded as if Colby had regained some of his strength and was using something to batter the door panels.

"Quick. Hurry," said Max. "He might get through the door soon."

"What's your name?" she asked him again.

"Max Deardon."

"I've typed into the system. We'll have someone with you shortly."

"Thanks." He replied then quickly terminated the call by putting the unit into the charger.

It was only then that he was aware that the sound of the thuds had ceased. Gingerly moving forward, he ventured out of the sitting room and advanced across the floor to the door leading into the kitchen. The bright interior light was still on, but there was no sound. He took a peek around the door frame, half expecting a crazed Colby to come flying at him.

The door leading into the cellar was open. The key was still on the other side, but there was a panel missing in the door. All he could assume was that Colby had managed to knock out the panel, put his hand through the opening and turn the key in the lock to open the door from the inside. He listened for any sound but couldn't hear a thing. He could make out the dots of red on the white tiled floor. He followed the trail which led out of the door.

He turned back out of the room, then was aware of the sound of steps on the stairs going up to the upper floor. Colby came tearing around the corner and vaulted towards him. Something he was holding in his left hand flashed. It had a silver coating. It was the blade of a knife. Colby lunged at him, but Max was able to swivel his body and get out of the way of the attack. Colby lunged at him for a second time, Max raised his hands and set himself in a defensive posture. As Colby came towards him he seemed to misjudge his movement.

Max grasped his chance. He reached out and was able to wrap both his hands around Colby's left-hand wrist and force it down. Colby was severely weakened by the wound to his right arm. He couldn't summon the strength to fight. He let go of the knife, which he must have got from a kitchen drawer. It fell to the tiled floor with a solid clink. Max had the advantage. He swung his right arm elbow into Colby's face and whacked it against his nose.

With the knife on the floor he was able to kick it and send it skidding across the tiled surface like an ice hockey puck. He let go of Colby's left hand and elbowed him for a second time, this time in the chest which sent him crashing against the wall. He fell to the floor in a heap.

He had managed to get the scalpel out of his arm, but blood was still leaking out of the open wound. There was a wan pallor to his skin. His face was glinting with perspiration. He looked at the wound and the stream of matted blood. The fight had gone from him. Nevertheless, Max stayed on the defensive and ready to react should he try to get off the floor and come at him again. From the resigned look on Colby's face it didn't look as if he would try again.

"Why are you fighting?" Max asked. Colby ignored him. "It's over," said Max. Again, Colby didn't reply.

A few long moments of silence passed, then the house was filled with the sound of a ringing telephone.

"I'm not answering that," said Max. The telephone rang at least a dozen times with a shrilling tone. "The police are on their way," said Max. "They'll fix you up and get you off to casualty. You'll be okay," he said.

The telephone stopped. Several moments passed before it started again.

"That will be Helena," Colby said.

"How do you know?"

"I sense it."

The phone stopped ringing after seven or eight times. Colby tried to raise himself off the floor but couldn't muster the energy to get up. He was wincing and taking in deep gulps of air. Max just hoped that the police would arrive sooner rather than later.

"You'll be okay," he repeated. "They'll take you to A and E. You'll recover in time."

"What'll I do? Twenty years?" Colby asked. His voice was weak. He may have been going into shock due to the loss of blood.

"No idea," said Max.

Colby didn't seem like the kind of person who could do prison time. He was too comfortable, too pampered. He would have a job to cope with the everyday monotony of prison life. A tear of moisture came from his eye and ran down his cheek.

He winched. "I've really fucked up."

"Tell it to the judge," said Max.

"They'll be no trial."

He sounded as if he was on the edge. A few moments of silence passed. The chime of the clock on the mantel piece rang quarter to eleven. Max remained by the door to the kitchen watching over Colby, just waiting for the police to arrive. Nothing more was said.

# Chapter 21

The first of two police cars arrived at the house at around five to eleven. The pale yellow and blue livery on the car said: Thames Valley Police.

The first one despatched two uniformed officers on the scene. Max let them into the house. They came down the hallway, into the reception area and clapped their eyes on the bloodied Colby propped up against the wall. The younger one of the police officers made an 'Oh My God' face.

"What happened here?" he asked is older, more experienced colleague.

"It's a long story," Max said.

"Keep it short," he advised.

Max told him how he had come to see his brother-in-law and how Colby had first drugged him with something in a drink, then how he had strapped him to a dentist chair that was downstairs in the cellar. The police officers asked Max several questions which he was able to answer.

A second car arrived, several minutes after the first one, with two more uniformed constables. A third car arrived moments after the second one. It was a grey Volkswagen Passat that brought DIs Rogerson and Skinner to the house.

The DIs took Max to aside and asked him to tell them what had happened. While he was talking to the plain-clothed guys, the uniformed officers were administering basic first-aid to Colby. A paramedic had been called.

Max told DI Rogerson and DI Skinner what Colby had told him about the dead girl and the other two unknown men who had been killed in the house and were now buried in shallow graves in the field at the bottom the hill. DI Skinner made a few phone calls. One call was to DI Welsh.

DI Rogerson asked Max to show them the room in the cellar. He obliged. He took them into the kitchen, through the smashed door, down the steps and into the room that was set up like a dental surgery. The sight amazed them. He showed them the snapped wrist restraint and the strap used to secure his head to the headrest. The syringe Colby had used to inject him with a drug was on the floor along with the other implements that had fallen off the tray. He showed them the red mark on his upper arm where Colby had injected him. His t-shirt was on a seat. DI Skinner retrieved it and passed it to Max. He slipped it on over his head.

Once the officers had seen enough, they all went back up into the kitchen then through into the reception area. The uniformed police officers had managed to get a bandage, made of paper kitchen towel, around Colby's arm. They had succeeded in stopping the flow of blood and cleaning the wound.

The next vehicle to arrive was a female paramedic. She went straight to Colby to deal with the cut and bandage his arm. The two uniformed constables were lingering by the front door.

After a further five minutes Colby was placed into the paramedic's car, which left the house for the local hospital, escorted by one of the marked police cars.

The car carrying Colby to hospital had not been gone long before another car pulled onto the pebble courtyard next to Max's car. This one was a metallic silver Vauxhall Astra.

DI Welsh and DI Malik emerged and were caught in the lights flashing from the police cars. They came into the house and were joined by DI Rogerson and DI Skinner. The four of them quickly got together and became involved in a conversation. DI Rogerson did most of the talking. He explained to them what he had been met with when he arrived on the scene and what Max had told him.

DI Welsh emerged out of the sitting room followed by DI Malik. Rogerson and Skinner were loitering by the sitting room door, while the other two uniformed officers were going from room to room to conduct a search of the house.

DI Welsh approached Max. "What happened?" she asked.

Max told her, relaying almost word for word what he had first told the uniformed guys, then Rogerson and Skinner. He told her how Colby had opened up to him and admitted that he had strangled a girl he met at a sex party given by Louis Delaney, how her body was buried in the wood, then how Colby had tortured two men on Delaney's say-so, before they were shot and buried in the same place.

The detectives listened to every word. Maybe they were checking to see if it was the same story he had told Rogerson and Skinner. It was. He told them he had, earlier in the day, spoken to his sister on the telephone. Then how he had called Colby from home and arranged to come and see him.

DI Welsh informed Max the team searching for bodies in the field, had, in the past two hours, located one badly decomposed corpse. She didn't know if the body was male or female. It was too early to tell. Only when a pathologist had examined the remains would they know for certain.

Max looked out of the open door at the continuous flash of red, blue, and white lights reflecting on the ground and up the brick wall. The telephone sounded once again.

"May I?" asked Max looking at the plain-clothed officers. DI Rogerson gave him permission to answer it. Max stepped into the sitting room, followed by Rogerson and Welsh. He picked up the receiver from the charger unit.

"Hello."

"Is that you Ralph?" asked a voice. It was Helena.

"He's not here," Max replied.

"Who is it?" she asked.

"It's Max."

"Where's Ralph?"

"He's not here."

"Where is he?"

"Helena. I think you'd better come home," said Max. "Straight away."

"Why. What's happened?"

"He's been hurt."

"Is it serious?" she asked.

"He's on his way to hospital."

"Oh, my word," she said. Max didn't reply. There was a sound of a raised voice from one of the policemen in the house. Helena could hear it. "Who's in the house?" she asked.

"The police."

"Oh my God. How badly is he hurt?"

"He's not in danger."

"Can you collect me from Kings Cross? I'm just coming into London," she said.

"Of course, I can."

"Can you take me straight to where he is?"

"Yes. I think that would be okay."

"I'll be able to see him. Won't I?"

"I would think so."

Then the line broke-up as the train must have entered into one of the rail tunnels on the outskirts of the city. Then she came back on as the signal was restored.

"Is he in trouble?" she asked.

"Yes. I think that's a fair assessment." She sighed. "I'll get there as soon as possible," he said.

"Okay. See you soon." She ended the call.

Max put the unit back into the charger and looked at DI Welsh. She looked at him fleetingly, then turned away from him to join her colleagues in the kitchen.

Max took his jacket and put it over his shoulders. He walked out of the sitting room, through the house and out into the forecourt. Now he had to drive into central London to collect Helena. He'd have a lot of explaining to do. He wasn't looking forward to it.

THE END

Printed in Great Britain
by Amazon